Jitters

JITTERS

a play by David French

Talonbooks • Vancouver • 1986

published with assistance from the Canada Council

Talonbooks
201 / 1019 East Cordova
Vancouver
British Columbia V6A 1M8
Canada

Typeset in Baskerville by Pièce de Résistance; printed and bound in Canada by Hignell Printing Ltd.

First printing: June 1980
First printing (revised edition): September 1986
Second printing: September 1991

Jitters was first published by Playwrights Co-op, Toronto, Ontario.

Canadian Cataloguing in Publication Data

French, David, 1939—
  Jitters

  A play.
  ISBN 0-88922-242-8

  I. Title.
PS8561.R4J6 1986   C812'.54   C86-091459-3
PR9199.3.F74J6 1986

to Sean Sullivan

Jitters was first performed at Tarragon Theatre in Toronto, Ontario on Feburary 16, 1979, with the following cast:

Patrick	David Calderisi
Jessica	Charmion King
Phil	Les Carlson
George	Miles Potter
Robert	Matt Walsh
Tom	Jim Mezon
Nick	Morison Bock
Susi	Amanda Lewis
Peggy	Sheilah Currie

Directed by Bill Glassco
Designed by David Moe
Lighting by Robert Thompson

Jitters was also performed at the Long Wharf Theatre in New Haven, Connecticut on October 16, 1979, with the following cast:

Patrick	Roland Hewgill
Jessica	Charmion King
Phil	George Sperdakos
George	Jim Jansen
Robert	Josh Clark
Tom	Joel Polis
Nick	William Carden
Susi	Jane Galloway
Peggy	Sarah Chodoff

Directed by Bill Glassco
Designed by Eldon Elder
Costumes by Rachel Kurland
Lighting by Jamie Gallagher

The Characters

Patrick Flanagan
Jessica Logan
Phil Mastorakis
George Ellsworth
Robert Ross
Tom Kent
Nick
Susi
Peggy

Act One

An afternoon in May

Act Two

Four days later

Act Three

The next afternoon

Act One

The set of the play-within-the-play, although the audience is as yet unaware of this. The set is the living-room of a middle-class home. There is a sofa, armchair, hi-fi, hanging plants and a Christmas tree. In the hallway a staircase leads up to the second floor. The front door is offstage.

The time of the play-within-the-play is winter. This particular scene takes place at night.

At rise, JESSICA is seated on the sofa, knitting with the sort of concentration that is an attempt to hide anxiety.

At the table, PHIL and TOM have just finished a hand of gin. While TOM shuffles the cards, PHIL pours himself a glass of Scotch.

JESSICA:
What time is it?

PHIL:
It's almost midnight. I don't think he'll be back.

JESSICA:
I keep thinking I hear his car.

Slight pause.

PHIL:
Can I get you something?

JESSICA:
I'm fine.

PHIL:
You sure, Sis? It's no trouble.

JESSICA:
Eric, I said no. I'm in no mood to drink. Just leave me alone.

TOM:
Oh, for Christ's sake, Mom!

He hurls the cards down on the table, rises, and crosses to stage left where he stands shuffling his feet.

JESSICA: *to TOM*
Watch your temper, you. I won't have that sort of language in this house.

TOM:
That's funny, coming from you.

JESSICA:
When have you heard me talk like that? I have never used that sort of language. Ever.

PHIL:

Come on, you two. Haven't we had enough for one night?

TOM.

He's making a fool of you, Mom, and you're the only one who can't see it. Frank's only out for what he can get.

JESSICA:

Aren't we all?

TOM:

Haven't you ever wondered where he goes every Thursday afternoon? Or do you prefer not to know?

PHIL:

Please, Jimmy, this isn't the time.

JESSICA: *to TOM*

What are you getting at?

TOM:

He goes to 438 Duncan Street. He takes a key from under the mat and lets himself in.

JESSICA:

How do you know?

TOM:

I followed him.

PHIL:

Jimmy, you promised you wouldn't...

TOM: *cutting in*

You want to know who lives at 438 Duncan Street? An eighteen-year-old girl who waits on tables at the Horse's Ass.

11

PHIL:
>The what?

JESSICA:
>I think he said the Horse's Ass.

>*They all break up.*

GEORGE: *from his seat in the audience*
>All right, cast, we'll stop there. We'll run it from the top
>now in costume.

TOM:
>Sorry, George. I know it's the Horse's Head. I don't
>know why I said the Horse's Ass.

GEORGE:
>Just don't say it tonight, Tom.   *calling out*
>Patrick, we're not going on. We won't be needing you.

PATRICK: *entering*
>I could've told you that weeks ago. From now on I'll
>phone in my part.

>*PEGGY enters from backstage and begins to set up for the
>top of the play.*

GEORGE:
>How was it that time, Jess? Did the knitting help?

JESSICA:
>It's perfect. Exactly what a woman might do if she's
>anxious.

GEORGE:
>You sure, love?

JESSICA:
>Absolutely. I know what I do: I clean the oven or wax
>the floor.

PATRICK:

Just don't get too excited when you rush out to greet me. I don't want a knitting needle in my eye.

He sits

JESSICA:

Worry more about the critics, Flanagan. They go straight for the jugular without dropping a stitch.

PATRICK:

I'd rather worry about my acting, if you don't mind.

JESSICA:

I can understand that. I'd be worried, too, if I were you.

PATRICK:

Exactly what does that mean?

JESSICA:

Not now, darling. I know a good exit line when I hear it.

She exits.

TOM:

How's my position, George? It always feels... you know... like I'm too far stage left.

GEORGE:

No, I want the distance. Only don't shuffle your feet. It looks like you're doing a soft shoe.

TOM:

I'm expressing my anxiety.

PATRICK:

Why don't you have him clean the oven or wax the floor?

GEORGE:

Tom, it's better to remain still. Especially when Jess is speaking. At that moment the focus should be on her and you take it away if you move.

PATRICK: *to TOM*

In other words, you're upstaging our Star. Cut it out.

TOM: *to GEORGE*

I won't do it again. I promise.

He exits.

GEORGE starts down the aisle.

NICK: *over the PA*

A run-through of the show will begin in twenty minutes. Please be ready to go at four o'clock. Peggy, be set as soon as you can.

PHIL:

George, old buddy, have you seen my costume? My so-called costume?

GEORGE: *stepping onstage*

What's wrong with it?

PHIL:

It's hideous. I'm insulted. Deeply offended.

GEORGE:

Put it on, Phil. Let's have a look.

He sits at the table and takes a sandwich out of his lunch bag.

PHIL:

George, you're a wonderful man, a sweetheart. I'd do anything for you. Anything. Even take my shirt off on stage. But don't ask me to be more ridiculous than that.

He exits backstage.

PATRICK:

> I'm waiting. And don't tell me again she didn't mean it. That's the second time in two days.

GEORGE: *eating the sandwich*

> I still think it was an accident.

PATRICK:

> Don't give me that. That apron is supposed to hit my chest, not my face. She threw it so hard it knocked my hat off.

GEORGE:

> That part I don't like. But your reaction was marvellous.

PATRICK:

> What reaction?

GEORGE:

> The way you raised your fist.

PATRICK:

> That was my own reaction, not the character's.

GEORGE:

> Keep it. And I loved that little dance you did. Like you were holding the lid on a volcano.

PATRICK:

> That wasn't *acting*, mate. I wanted to punch her in the mouth. Knock her right on her twelve-carat arse.

GEORGE:

> Patrick, the tension was terrific. I wasn't sure whether you were going to hit her or not. Believe me, the audience will feel that, too.

PATRICK:
> I'll let you in on a little secret. You listening? If she
> throws that apron in my face one more time, I won't
> leave you or the audience in any doubt. Is that too
> subtle for you?

SUSI: *entering*
> George, treasure, I hate to interrupt but since I'm such
> a good sport I've volunteered to work on my tea-break.

GEORGE:
> What is it, Susi?

SUSI:
> The sofa cushion needs mending. Would you mind if I
> did it now? I'm in a hurry.

GEORGE:
> Now or later, love. But it has to be done by tonight.

> *PATRICK rises and crosses to the table.*

GEORGE:
> Sorry. Where were we?

> *SUSI sits on the sofa and mends the cushion.*

PATRICK:
> We were talking about that prima donna. Canada's
> Own Jessica Logan. God, that kills me. She's been in
> the States half her life, she comes home to do one play
> for six weeks, and suddenly she's a national resource.

GEORGE:
> Blame the press, not her. You know what they're like.

PATRICK:
> I've been a name here for twenty years, I can't even get
> a bank loan.

GEORGE:

You want a sandwich?

PATRICK:

Even in that Albee piece she played herself. That's all she can do, bitches.

GEORGE:

I made it myself. Cheddar cheese on pumpernickel.

PATRICK:

Bitches and tarts. That's her forte. Middle-aged bitches and sleazy tarts.

GEORGE:

Pat, she's not playing a bitch. This is a very sympathetic role.

PATRICK:

And smaller than mine. And for that she gets top billing. I have to squint to read my name on the posters.

GEORGE:

Look, I know you two aren't exactly hitting it off, but your work together is sensational. I'm very happy. So is Robert.

PATRICK:

Well, he has a funny way of showing it, our playwright. Most days he slinks in here and broods. His silences are right out of Pinter.

GEORGE:

He's just shy. It's only his second play.

PATRICK:

Today's the first time he's spoken to me all week. Come to think of it, I prefer his silences. No, really, he has no tact, that kid. So keep him away from me. As far as possible.

PHIL: *off*

George, I'm dressed. Are you ready for this?

GEORGE:

Just a minute, Phil.   *to PATRICK*   Look, we'll talk about this later, okay?

PATRICK:

I'm a damned fine actor, and he ought to consider himself lucky to get me. Instead he picks away at my confidence. Well, this's the last play of his I'm ever going to do, and you can tell him that for me.

He exits backstage.

SUSI: *still mending the cushion*

He's really on the warpath, isn't he? I'm glad I kept my mouth shut.

PEGGY:

That's the first time he's attacked Robert. I'm surprised.

GEORGE:

Well, it's the first preview tonight. That might have something to do with it.

PHIL: *off*

George, I'm still here. I haven't got all day.

GEORGE:

Whenever you're ready, Phil.

PHIL enters, dressed as a priest.

18

PHIL:

Well?

GEORGE:

You look great. What's the problem?

PHIL:

Are you kidding? Look how tight the pants are. The man's a priest, not a flamenco dancer. What priest wears tight pants? Not only is it sacrilegious, it's worse—it's ludicrous.

GEORGE:

They don't look that tight.

PHIL:

No, not if I'm dancing *Swan Lake*. George, old buddy, this is a contemporary play. You want me in this costume? Fine. Give me a rapier and change my lines to iambic pentameter.

GEORGE:

How is it otherwise?

PHIL:

See for yourself. Not only are the pants tight, they're shiny. Is this man so poor he has to iron his own pants?

GEORGE:

Is that it?

PHIL:

No, this clerical collar's too small. My neck's 15½, this collar's 14. We've got four previews, George. Four previews starting tonight. By the opening my eyes'll bug out so much they'll think I have a thyroid condition.

GEORGE:

What else, Phil?

PHIL:

Isn't that enough?

GEORGE:

All right, I'll see what I can do. Thanks.

PHIL: *as he starts to exit*

I won't even mention the shoes.

GEORGE:

What's wrong with the shoes?

PHIL: *stopping*

The right one pinches.

GEORGE:

Why just the right?

PHIL:

My right foot's one inch longer than my left.
He points at SUSI. And no jokes.

GEORGE:

All right, I'll talk to Wardrobe, they must've forgotten.
We don't want you mincing in this role.

PHIL:

And one last thing, George. Bear with me on this.

GEORGE:

What?

PHIL:

Believe me, I don't want to be difficult. I hesitate even
to mention it, it's the hairpiece. I ask you, what priest
wears a toupee?

SUSI:

A priest with tight pants.

PHIL: *to GEORGE*

You see that? From the mouth of babes, George. From the mouth of babes   *to SUSI*   Thank you, sweetheart.

GEORGE:

Listen, I was against the hairpiece from the start. It was your idea.

PHIL:

Okay, so I changed my mind. It looks tacky. Besides, who the hell needs a rug? I can *act* hair!

He exits backstage.

SUSI:

He's making the girls in Wardrobe rich. They've never had so much overtime.

GEORGE: *to the control booth*

Nick, did you get all that?   *then*   Nick?

PEGGY:

He may have gone for a coffee.

GEORGE:

Then tell Wardrobe to take Phil's pants away for the run-through.

PEGGY:

There's nothing wrong with his pants.

GEORGE:

I know that, but let him think they've been worked on. He'll drive us crazy, otherwise.

He has finished eating. He crumples the paper bag and tosses it off the stage.

Enter TOM.

TOM:

Susi, do you think I could have two comps for tomorrow night? My Dad can't make the opening.

SUSI:

No problem. I'll leave two tickets at the box office in your name.

TOM:

Great. Thanks.

SUSI:

And next time you want a favour, Tom, drop by my apartment. We'll talk about it in the shower.

TOM:

Is she kidding, George? I never know when she's kidding.

PEGGY:

She's not kidding, Tom. Her water bill's higher than her rent.

GEORGE:

Let's skip hygiene for now, Tom. Sit down.
TOM does.   Tell me, how's Jess?

TOM:

Oh, I think she's fabulous. She's so generous. So easy to work with...

GEORGE:

No, I mean how's she holding up? It's hard to know with Jess. Did she say anything at lunch?

TOM:

She's not showing it, George, but she's really upset. Like, she kept dropping her knife and fork. Things like that.

GEORGE:
  What else?

TOM:
  She wouldn't eat her sandwich. Luigi made it with
  mayonnaise and she made him take it back. Jess never
  complains like that, even when the toast is burnt.

SUSI:
  Is Patrick still calling her at three in the morning?

TOM:
  Yeah, he is. I told her she should take her phone off.

PEGGY:
  And did she?

TOM:
  Yeah, she did. And two nights running he called the guy
  next door. He said it was an emergency, her phone was
  off the hook, and could he run next door and tell her.

GEORGE: *rising*
  Jesus, he's impossible.

TOM:
  I know. Now the guy next door has *his* phone off the
  hook. So like, last night, guess what happens?

GEORGE:
  What?

TOM:
  Around three or four in the morning, she said, a pizza
  truck pulls up in front of her house.

GEORGE:
  A pizza truck?

23

TOM:

She says if he gets any more smart ideas and sends an ambulance, she'll go him one better and take it. Then he'll be up a creek.

SUSI:

Won't we all?

GEORGE:

Okay, thanks, Tom. You better finish dressing.   *TOM is staring at SUSI.*   Tom.

TOM:

Oh. You bet.

He exits.

NICK: *over the PA*
Peggy, have you finished your preset?

PEGGY:

George, is that where you want the armchair? You better double-check. Yes, Nick, we're all set.

GEORGE: *to PEGGY*
That's perfect. Would you tell the cast I want to speak to them onstage before the run-through? And tell Jess and Patrick to come out as soon as they're ready.

PEGGY:

I'll hurry them up.

GEORGE:

One more thing. Any sign of a bottle?
PEGGY shakes her head.   Well, keep checking the dressing-room. If you find anything, let me know.

PEGGY:

Actors who drink make me nervous.

SUSI:
Actors who drink and make phone calls at three a.m. make me glad I'm front-of-house. I wouldn't want to be on stage with one.

PEGGY:
I like Patrick, though. I know he's a bastard, but he's very sensitive.

She exits backstage.

SUSI:
Oh, God, not one of those types. Is she in the right business.

PEGGY: *returning*
Besides, I don't think Patrick even remembers those calls. If he did, how could he look anyone in the eye?

She exits.

SUSI:
I bet she picks up stray puppies. There. I'm finished, George. Anything else I can do?

GEORGE:
Yes, I want you on book for the run-through. Robert's been bitching again. He's worried about the text.

SUSI:
George, I don't have all that much time. I still have to clean the lobby and washrooms.

GEORGE:
Get one of the other girls to do that. This is more important. The actors really are getting sloppy. Phil is the worst.

SUSI:

I can believe that. I've been running lines with him. I know them better than he does.

GEORGE:

How's the house?

SUSI:

We're sold out. A waiting list of thirty-five, last time I checked. And the word from New York is good. Bernie Feldman is definitely coming.

GEORGE:

His office confirmed it?

SUSI:

This morning. He'll be here for the opening. So cheer up, treasure. We just might be making headlines.

She exits.

GEORGE: *to the control booth*
Nick, are you in the booth?

NICK: *over the PA*
I'm here.

GEORGE:

Good. I want to make a change in the sound level at the top of the show. It's too loud. What is it now?

NICK:

It's at four.

GEORGE:

Bring it down to three and a half. You got that?

NICK:

Yeah, I got it.

GEORGE:

And I want the music in faster. As soon as the house goes to half, bring it in and up. Don't wait.

NICK:

I wish you'd make up your mind. This morning you told me to go to black before I bring in the music.

GEORGE:

That's what run-throughs are for, Nick. So I can change my mind. I may even change it again before we open. Now did you get that?   *then*   Nick?

NICK:

What? The new cue or the sarcasm?

ROBERT enters down the aisle, carrying two cups of coffee in styrofoam cups.

GEORGE:

Oh, hi, Robert. I thought you'd left.

ROBERT: *suspiciously*

Why? Did you want me to?

GEORGE:

No, of course not. Listen, did you say anything to Patrick today? Anything that might upset him?

He takes a coffee.

ROBERT:

I said hello, that's all. Why? Did he say I upset him?

GEORGE:

No, but he's got this idea in his head you don't like what he's doing. I thought maybe you knew why.

27

ROBERT:

Jesus, I think it's the best thing he's ever done. I couldn't be more pleased. I love to come in here and just watch him work.

GEORGE:

Don't tell me, tell him.

ROBERT:

I couldn't.

GEORGE:

Why not?

ROBERT:

I couldn't say things like that to his face, I'd be too embarrassed. Besides, it's Jess I'm worried about. She was terrible today.

GEORGE:

I know. All of a sudden she's playing emotions instead of objectives.

ROBERT:

What're you going to do about it?

GEORGE:

Well, it's only been the last couple of days. I'll see what happens in the run-through. Meanwhile, do me a favour: stay out of his way; don't even look at him.

ROBERT:

Yeah, and then he'll think for sure I don't like him.

GEORGE:

Now you know what I go through. If I spend too much time with Jess, he says I'm neglecting him. If I do give him special attention, he gets insecure and says, ''Why don't you work with her? She's the one who needs it.''

ROBERT:
    Be firm. You're the director. Either he gets his act
    together

GEORGE: *cutting in*
    Or what? If I lay down the law, he might quit. It's four
    days to opening. You want that?   *ROBERT says
    nothing.*   He knows damn well we can't replace him.
    He thinks he can pull any stunt now and get away
    with it.

ROBERT:
    That's even more reason to be firm, isn't it? What if
    Jess decides she can't take any more? What then?

GEORGE:
    She won't.

ROBERT:
    How do you know?

GEORGE:
    Robert, listen to me. She chose this play. It was her idea
    to do it in Toronto and get a New York producer up.

ROBERT:
    So?

GEORGE:
    So she's not about to let Patrick botch her chance to
    take this show to Broadway.

ROBERT:
    Yeah, but how much can she put up with?

GEORGE:
    A lot. He may be difficult but he's worth it. The best
    scenes in the play are the ones they have together.

ROBERT:

They also happen to be the best-written.

GEORGE:

I'm not saying they're not. All I'm saying is he gives her a lot to work with. In other words, he's good for the *play*. And what's good for the play is good for her, for me, and for you. *You*, Robert.

Enter JESSICA followed by PATRICK. She is now wearing a curly blond wig.

JESSICA:

George, I want your unbiased opinion. Does this wig look funny?

GEORGE:

It doesn't look funny. It looks stunning.

PATRICK: *to JESSICA*

I never said the wig looked funny. I said you looked funny in the wig. Hello, Robert. Still waiting to see if I improve?

JESSICA:

He'll have a helluva long wait if your talent's as limp as your wit.   *to GEORGE*   What can we do for you, darling? Peggy said you wanted to see us.

NICK: *over the PA*

Top of Act One in five minutes, please.

GEORGE:

I want to go over a moment in the second act. There seems to be a slight problem.

JESSICA:

What moment's that?

GEORGE:
The bit with the apron.

PATRICK:
Oh, *that* moment.

JESSICA:
I thought that moment worked quite well for me.

PATRICK:
I think that's the problem.

GEORGE:
I don't want anyone to get hurt. So let's take a look at it. Jess, are you hitting your mark?

JESSICA:
I always hit my mark.

PATRICK:
Notice how she looks my way? Try to be a little more subtle, love. In the trade we call that "indicating."

JESSICA:
Yes, I know. I saw your Shylock.

GEORGE:
What about you, Patrick? It seems to me you were a little too far upstage of the table.

PATRICK:
Well, I hate to contradict the director, but I was standing exactly where I always stand.

GEORGE:
Okay, let's see your positions. That way I can judge for myself.

He goes up the aisle.

PATRICK and JESSICA take their positions upstage of the table.

PATRICK:
Here it is I haven't budged since we blocked it

GEORGE:
Are you in position, Jess?

JESSICA:
I am.

       TOM rushes on, dressed in yellow polo pajamas.

TOM:
Do you need me, George? Peggy said you were doing the apron scene.

GEORGE:
No, I don't need you, Tom. Thanks, anyway.
TOM exits.   Patrick, maybe if you moved a step or two closer she'd be more certain of her aim.

PATRICK:
If it's a question of aim, I'd prefer to stand in the wings, if you don't mind.

JESSICA:
Aren't you being paranoid? It was an accident.

PATRICK:
Listen, that was no accident. Once is an accident. Twice is assault with intent to wound. Is that the best you could dream up, an apron in the face?

JESSICA:
No, but then it's not four in the morning, is it? Which reminds me. Next time you order pizza, make it a small without anchovies.

PATRICK:
What're you talking about?

JESSICA:
And call the same place. I adored that curly-haired delivery boy.

PATRICK:
I don't know what she's talking about. She's crazy.

GEORGE:
Please, Jess, Patrick, the moment's not that important.   *to JESSICA*   From now on just toss the apron at his feet. That'll make the same point.

ROBERT reacts to this.

PATRICK:
Fine, but I won't pick it up.

GEORGE:
I'm not asking you to. Tom's in the scene, I'll have him pick it up.

ROBERT:
Wait a minute, George. Don't you think that weakens the moment? It's much stronger if she hits him.

PATRICK:
Listen, boyo, one moment's not going to make or break your precious play, so don't get defensive. I don't care what the script says, I'm not getting an apron snapped in my face. Is that understood?

He exits.

JESSICA:
Adamant, isn't he? That's what I like, a man who knows what he doesn't want.   *to ROBERT*   Give me a cigarette, darling.

ROBERT does, and lights it for her.

JESSICA: *as GEORGE comes down the aisle*
Don't worry: no more aprons in the hair. I've gotten it
out of my system. But God, it felt good. I could've done
that all day.

ROBERT:
I don't blame you.

JESSICA: *sitting at the table*
What was he like in your first play, Robert? Was he
much trouble?

ROBERT:
No, but in *Murphy's Diamond* he had top billing. Besides,
he always gets along much better with...   *He stops,*
realizing he's almost put his foot in his mouth.   ... you
know... with...   *He looks desperately to GEORGE for*
help.

JESSICA:
With what? Young actors?

GEORGE: *quickly, as he steps onstage*
I don't think that's what Robert meant. I think he
means actors like Tom. Kids he doesn't feel threatened
by. You know.   *He gives ROBERT a throat-cutting*
gesture.   Pat better watch out, though. He's getting a
reputation for being temperamental.

JESSICA:
Don't kid yourself. Any actor as good as Flanagan
always works. But right now I want to talk about me,
not him. How'm I doing, George? I can't tell any more.
I feel I'm not doing justice to the woman.

GEORGE:

It's coming along beautifully. Isn't it Robert? God, the improvement today in the second act was phenomenal. It's not quite there, granted, but you have no need to worry.

JESSICA:

I've been away two years, George. I'm rusty. I can't seem to relax and enjoy it.

GEORGE:

You tell her, Robert. She's wonderful, isn't she?

ROBERT:

It's a much tougher role than Flanagan's. He has the far more colourful character.

JESSICA:

Oh? You think so?

GEORGE:

I think what Robert means is that you're very close to this character, and that's hard to play. Whereas Patrick's role is a character role. Isn't that what you meant, Robert?

JESSICA:

George, the last two directors I worked with didn't have the guts to level with me, and one was my ex. I would've been better if they'd been more honest.

GEORGE:

I'm being as honest as I know how.

JESSICA:

I want this play to work for me. I'm counting on it. What I don't need is to be told I'm marvellous when I'm not.

GEORGE:

Jess, you're one of the best actresses this country's ever produced. Look at the work you've done in London and New York. My God, most actors would sell out their country to have worked with Olivier.

JESSICA:

Is that what you think I've done? Sold out?

GEORGE:

No, no. Look, we've all been under a strain the past few days. Once we get in front of an audience Patrick will start to behave himself.

JESSICA:

Patrick? Well, if you think Patrick's affecting my performance you better do something about it and damn quick.

Enter PHIL and TOM.

PHIL:

Here we are, friends. "The brief abstracts and chroniclers of our time."

TOM:

What's that from?

PHIL:

Hamlet.

TOM:

Did you do *Hamlet*?

PHIL:

Are you kidding? I've done all the classics.

TOM:

Who'd you play, Osric?

PHIL:

No, the grave-digger.

GEORGE:

Don't believe him. He did the Player Queen and he was damn good, too. He only did the grave-digger one night. Where's Patrick?

PATRICK: *entering*

Coming.

> *PATRICK sits at the table. PEGGY enters and also sits at the table. JESSICA and TOM sit on the sofa. PHIL moves to the armchair and ROBERT to the window seat. GEORGE remains on his feet.*

NICK: *over the PA*

George, we have two and a half hours to have this run. If you want the actors to have a proper dinner break, we have to start right away.

GEORGE: *to the control booth*

This'll only take two minutes.

NICK:

We don't have two minutes.

GEORGE:

Then we'll make two minutes, won't we? ...Okay, let's settle down. I just want to say a few words. First, I think you'll all agree we made enormous progress today with Act Two. Some exciting things were beginning to happen. I know you all felt that.   *Slight pause.*   You did all feel that, didn't you? I thought the last scene was stupendous. It still needs toning down, but it was really beginning to cook.

PHIL:

George, I still don't have the new shoes. Have you spoken to Wardrobe?

GEORGE:

No, I haven't had time. I promise you'll have them for tonight. Peggy, make a note of that. Phil has to have new shoes.   *to the control booth*   Nick, did you hear that?

NICK: *over the PA*
What size?

PHIL:

A nine and a ten.

NICK:

Come again.

GEORGE:

He needs two different sizes. One foot's a bit longer than the other.   *to PHIL*   Actually, you only need one shoe, don't you? The left foot?

PHIL:

No, the right.   *to NICK*   A size ten for the right foot, sweetheart. And make sure they match. I don't want the audience staring at my feet.

GEORGE:

Okay, let's go on. Where was I? ...Oh, yeah. Right now the show's running at least ten minutes too long. We can slash five minutes off tonight by just picking up cues. But don't rush it. Take your beats, take your pauses, but come in sharp on the cues. That's especially true at the beginning. It's important that we get off to a fast start with this play. A lot depends on your energy to drive it forward. Now, you've got four previews. Start working with the audience. By the time we open you'll have the right pace.

PATRICK:

Speaking of openings, what's the word from Mecca? Is Feldman coming?

GEORGE:
  He'll be here for sure, Pat. We just had word today.

PHIL:
  Beautiful!

TOM:
  Hollywood, here I come!

PATRICK:
  God, we're such a bunch of hicks. Let a Yankee
  producer notice and we all sit up and wag our tails.
  Well, he's not going to pick all of us. We know who'll
  get the nod and it won't be the men.

JESSICA:
  Nonsense. If Bernie likes the production, he'll move it
  intact.

TOM:
  Why wouldn't he like it? It's a super show.

PHIL:
  It's an incredible show. He'd have to be a Philistine.

PATRICK:
  With any luck, he'll give my role to George C. Scott.

NICK: *over the PA*
  Forgive me, cast, but can't we do that on the dinner
  break?

PATRICK:
  Which is fine by me. Not that I have anything against
  George C. Scott. It's just I'd rather work in Canada.
  Where else can you be a top-notch actor all your life
  and still die broke and anonymous?

PHIL:
  I can't even get arrested in this country.

GEORGE:

Okay, people, that's all for now. Are there any questions?

PATRICK:

Just one. *indicating PHIL* Does he really have one foot longer than the other?

He starts to exit.

PHIL:

I don't find that amusing.

PATRICK:

I doubt if your mother does, either, sweetheart. Must cost her a fortune to keep you in footwear.

He exits.

PHIL:

God, he's ridiculous. My mother hasn't bought my shoes in years.

NICK: *over the PA*

Top of Act One in five minutes, please.

JESSICA: *rising and crossing to GEORGE*

Interesting, isn't he?

GEORGE:

Who?

JESSICA:

Flanagan. I've never seen an actor so afraid.

GEORGE:

What? Afraid Feldman won't want him?

JESSICA:

No, Afraid that he will....Come along, Tommy. We've got work to do.

TOM.   *as he exits with JESSICA*

Jess, you know the first scene in Act Two? Does it sound funny the way I laugh? I find it hard to laugh on stage. Way harder than crying...

They exit.

GEORGE stands there, thinking about JESSICA's remark. PHIL is still seated in the armchair.

PEGGY:

Phil, places have been called.

PHIL:

One second, sweetheart. I want a word with George. Be right along.

PEGGY exits backstage.

GEORGE:

What's the problem?

PHIL:

I didn't want to bring this up in front of the others. Not around Flanagan.

He crosses to GEORGE.

GEORGE:

What is it?

PHIL:

I'm almost afraid to ask.

GEORGE:
   Don't be silly. What?

PHIL:
   Will there be a prompter for this show?

   He peers eagerly into GEORGE's face.

GEORGE:
   No. From tonight on you're all on your own out there.
   If you get in trouble, you'll just have to rely on each
   other.

PHIL:
   George, tell me you don't mean it. Tell me it's just your
   gallows humour. I can take a joke.

GEORGE:
   I'm sorry. We just don't have the staff. Besides, the
   theatre's too small. A prompter would be heard in the
   last row.

   He starts up the aisle.

PHIL:
   I'll tell you what else can be heard in the last row. An
   actor with his mouth open and no words coming out. Is
   that what you want? With Bernie Feldman squirming in
   his seat? I ask you?

ROBERT: *to GEORGE, quickly*
   I could prompt.

PHIL:
   God bless you.

GEORGE: *returning to the stage, to ROBERT*
I wouldn't let you within ten feet of the stage on
opening night. Look what happened at *Murphy's
Diamond*.

ROBERT:
Anyone can faint.

GEORGE:
Before the curtain goes up?

ROBERT:
What do you expect? It was my first play.

GEORGE:
That's right, and they weren't expecting anything. This
time they'll be waiting to see the whites of your eyes.

ROBERT:
Did you have to say that?

GEORGE:
I just don't want you crashing onto the set in a dead
swoon, so forget it. Look, Phil, you'll be great. I realize
you have a problem with the odd line, but by opening
night...   *PHIL is pacing, rubbing his
stomach.*   What's wrong?

PHIL:
It's nothing, nothing.

GEORGE:
Come on. What is it?

PHIL:
I don't want to burden you, George. It's nothing.
He winces.

GEORGE:
Phil, will you tell me what it is? Maybe I can help.

PHIL:

I think it's my ulcer.

GEORGE:

I never knew you had an ulcer.

PHIL:

Neither did I. Oh, the pain, the pain. Like a kidney stone.

NICK: *over the PA*

Should I get him a doctor?

PHIL:

No, a prompter!

GEORGE:

You don't need a prompter. That's all in your head. You just got off book this morning. The other actors've been off book for two weeks.

PHIL:

Sure, rub it in.

GEORGE:

I'm not. I'm just saying that's why you're a little unsure of the lines still. We've got four previews. By the time we open you'll be word perfect.

PHIL:

What if I dry?

GEORGE:

Why should you?

PHIL:

I always dry.

GEORGE:

That doesn't mean you will this time. Stop thinking that way.

PHIL.

George, I have long speeches in this play. Words coming out my ears. If I stumble, I could skip ten pages and not know it. You want ten minutes off the running time? I could easily slash twenty minutes off and still take all my beats and pauses.

ROBERT sits on the sofa and puts his face in his hands.

GEORGE:

Phil, you worry too much. You expect to dry, so you dry. Forget about the lines. I don't care if you get it word perfect. Neither does Robert. Isn't that so, Robert?

ROBERT nods, his face in his hands.

PHIL:

George, take part of my salary. Pay some kid to stand in the wings with a book. I'll buy the flashlight. Only don't take away my safety net. Look at me. Knots in my stomach, it's only a preview. Think how I'll be opening night. My throat tightens. My heart, George. My heart hammers so loud in my ears I sometimes miss my first cue.

GEORGE:

Calm down.

PHIL:

It's so bad I once thought of taking lip-reading.

GEORGE:

You're working yourself into a stew.

PHIL:

I know. And to look at me you'd think I had nerves of steel, right? "Phil," they say, "Phil, you're so relaxed on stage." Oh, if they only knew, George. If they only knew inside I'm twenty different flavours of Jello and a pulse rate of one hundred and forty.

NICK: *over the PA*

George, if Phil has recovered sufficiently I would like to get this show on the road. All actors should be in position. I would like the stage cleared.

> *ROBERT steps off the stage.*

GEORGE:

Sorry, Phil. We'll have to do this another time. Just don't underestimate yourself. You're a pro.

> *He takes his seat on the aisle.*

PHIL:

You bet your life I'm a pro. You think a novice like Tom would stand here pleading? Begging and grovelling? He hasn't had the experience. I know what it's like to be terrified: I'm a seasoned veteran. So bear that in mind when I implore you not to make me face the audience cold. Would you ask a man afraid of heights to jump from a plane without a parachute? God bless you, but there's a limit, George. A limit to what a man can do for Art. I'm only human. And don't hand me that crap you can't afford it. If you can afford to buy me shoes, you can afford a prompter.

NICK: *over the PA*

For the last time, can we please clear the stage? We'll be starting in one minute. That's sixty seconds.

> *Lights begin to dim and music starts.*

PHIL.,

I see I'm wasting my breath. Okay, have it your way
old buddy. *He starts to exit.* Just don't say I
never warned you. I love this play, and if I botch it, I'll
never forgive you. *He exits backstage, only to poke his
head out the window.* Look, George, hear me out. I
can't afford to screw up. Feldman's my only hope: he's
an American.

NICK:

Thirty seconds.

PHIL:

Down there they embrace success. Up here it's like
stepping out of line.

NICK:

Twenty seconds.

PHIL:

Don't you see? I may never get a break like this again.
That's all I'm saying.

NICK:

Fifteen.

PHIL:

You're all heart, Nick!

He exits.

ROBERT starts up the aisle and SUSI starts down.

SUSI: *to GEORGE*
Sorry, treasure, I was cleaning the lobby.

She sits in the aisle.

GEORGE:

Now remember: underline anything they get wrong, no matter how small. And if I'll there a line, give it to him.

> *The theatre is in blackness, except for the light of the flashlight.*

ROBERT:

Hey, George.

GEORGE:

What?

ROBERT:

Why do you think they're waiting to see the whites of my eyes?

GEORGE:

Robert, please! That was just a figure of speech!

> *Lights up onstage. JESSICA is alone onstage, watering the hanging plants. After a moment, PATRICK comes down the stairs. He is shirtless, and is doing up his belt. He glances at JESSICA, who ignores him. He crosses to the table and pours himself a cup of coffee.*

PATRICK: *with an Italian accent*

Why'd you get so upset for, Lizzie? All I asked is how long is he going to stay?

JESSICA:

He's home for the holidays. That's all I know. What do you want me to do, tell him to go to a hotel? He's my son.

PATRICK:

I don't like the way he looks at me. Like I'm not good enough to sit on the furniture. He'd better not start that today, because if he does, he'll wish like hell he didn't.

JESSICA:
I don't want trouble, Frank

PATRICK: *sitting at the table*
Then put his nose back in joint or I'll do it for him.

The doorbell rings.

JESSICA:
That's Eric, now.

She sets down the watering-can and switches off the hi-fi.

PATRICK:
Where the hell are my shoes?

JESSICA:
Honestly, you're worse than Jimmy.   *She stands behind his chair and strokes his chest.*   Your shoes are upstairs. And would you please put on a shirt?

PATRICK:
Lizzie, I'll give the kid two weeks. Either he's gone or I go. Make up your mind.

He rises.

JESSICA:
Don't threaten me.

PATRICK:
Two weeks, Lizzie.

He exits upstairs.

The doorbell rings again. JESSICA crosses into the hallway out of sight. We hear the door open and close.

PHIL: *off*
>   Hello, Elizabeth.

JESSICA: *off*
>   Hi, Eric. Come in. You look half-frozen.

>   *PHIL and JESSICA enter, PHIL taking off his overcoat. He glances into the living-room. He seems quite relieved to find it empty.*

>   Here. Let me take your coat.   *She hangs his hat, coat, and scarf on the hat rack.*   I appreciate this, Eric. I wouldn't have called if it wasn't important.

PHIL:
>   I know that. That's why I'm here.   *He crosses near the sofa.*   What is it? Frank?

JESSICA:
>   No, it's Jimmy.

PHIL:
>   Oh?

JESSICA:
>   Sit down. I just made a fresh pot of coffee. Have you eaten?

PHIL:
>   Nothing for me. I had breakfast at the rectory....What's happened, Sis?

JESSICA:
>   He's quit school.

PHIL:
>   Jimmy quit school?

>   *He sits on the sofa, near the arm.*

JESSICA:
>He says he's had all he can take of university and wants to stay here until he figures out what he's going to do.   *She sits on the arm of the sofa.*   I'd hate to see him make a mistake, Eric. I don't want him to do something he'll regret later on.

PHIL:
>Well, maybe university isn't what he needs right now.

JESSICA: *putting her hand on his knee*
>Please, I want you to talk to him. You're the only one who can. He won't listen to me.

PHIL:
>And how's Frank feel about all this?

JESSICA:
>He doesn't know yet. All he knows is Jimmy's home for the winter break.

>*PHIL nods. And nods. Clears his throat.*

GEORGE:
>Patrick, that was your cue.

PATRICK: *off*
>I beg to differ. My cue is Phil's line, "I see." I didn't hear it.

PHIL:
>I didn't say it.

GEORGE:
>Did you forget?

PHIL:
>No. I thought I'd try not saying it. Don't you feel the silence is more telling?

PATRICK: *off*

The only actor I know who likes to cut his lines.

PHIL:

That's because I can *act* them.

PATRICK: *off*

Act all you want, mate, only don't act my cues. I'll be up here all night.

GEORGE:

What do you think, Robert?

ROBERT:

Cut the line. He doesn't need it.

PHIL:

There. The author.

GEORGE:

Okay, Patrick, take your cue from Jessica's "Jimmy's home for the winter break." Jess, take it back to "Let me take your coat."

PHIL:

George, can I look away when she starts that crap about Jimmy? I did this time. It felt better.

GEORGE: *angrily*

Look, we can't have these interruptions! We have a preview tonight! Let's just get on with it! When you're ready, Jess. Thank you.

> *PHIL gives GEORGE a look. Then he and JESSICA get into position. He takes his overcoat off the hat rack and glances again at GEORGE.*

JESSICA:
Here. Let me take your coat   *PHIL thrusts it at her.*   I appreciate this, Eric. I wouldn't have called if it wasn't important.

PHIL: *irritably*
I know that. That's why I'm here.   *He crosses near the sofa.*   What is it? Frank?

JESSICA:
No, it's Jimmy.

PHIL:
Oh?

JESSICA:
Sit down. I just made a fresh pot of coffee. Have you eaten?

PHIL:
Nothing for me. I had brunch at the rectory...What's happened, Sis?

JESSICA:
He's quit school.

PHIL:
Jimmy's quit school?

He sits on the sofa, near the arm.

JESSICA:
He says he's had all he can take of university and wants to stay here until he figures out what he's going to do.   *She sits on the arm of the sofa.*   I'd hate to see him make a mistake, Eric. I don't want him to do something he'll regret later on.

PHIL:
   Well, maybe college isn't what he needs right now.

   He snoors out at L-H-I-R-I-R

JESSICA: *putting her hand on his knee*
   Please, I want you to talk to him. You're the only one
   who can. He won't listen to me.

PHIL:
   And how's Frank feel about all this?

JESSICA:
   He doesn't know yet. All he knows is Jimmy's home for
   the winter break.

   PATRICK comes down the stairs, laughing.

PHIL: *rising*
   Hello, Frank.

PATRICK: *to JESSICA*
   You ought to see that kid of yours. He can't even get
   his socks on. What, they don't teach him to drink in
   college?   *to PHIL*   So how's it going, Father? You
   still dipping into the poorbox?

JESSICA:
   Frank, you're awful.   *to PHIL*   He's just pulling
   your leg.

PHIL:
   Is he?

PATRICK:
   Did she tell you? The kid took a swing at me last night.

PHIL: *putting a cigarette in his mouth*
   No, Elizabeth never mentioned it...

He fishes in his pockets for matches.

PATRICK:
He thought he could drink me under the table.

He brings out his lighter and lights PHIL's cigarette.

PHIL:
Thanks....He's going through a very difficult period,
Jimmy.

PATRICK:
Well, he better get over it fast or he'll get his ass kicked.

JESSICA:
Frank, please.

PATRICK:
I mean it, Lizzie.

PHIL:
He needs understanding right now, not brute force.

PATRICK:
Is that so?

He sits on the sofa and stares at PHIL.

JESSICA: *moving behind PATRICK*
Honey, let Eric handle it. He knows how to talk to
Jimmy. Okay?

*She leans over to kiss the top of his head, but as she does
so, PATRICK ducks and leaps to his feet. He stares at
GEORGE, grimacing.*

GEORGE: *moving to the stage*
What's wrong?

PATRICK:

I don't like that kiss, I've never liked it, I can't do it.

GEORGE:

Patrick, we can't keep starting and stopping like this. We'll never get through the play.

PHIL:

How come *he* doesn't get hell? I notice you don't say he's interrupting. With him it's starting and stopping.

GEORGE: *to PATRICK*

What's wrong with the kiss?

PATRICK:

I don't believe her.

JESSICA:

Listen, you, I was doing leading ladies when you were failing to get through adolescence. So don't tell me how to act.

PATRICK:

I forgot: she's worked with Mike Nichols. Let's all curtsy.

JESSICA:

At least I've got the guts to work outside this country.

PATRICK:

The truth is your last two Broadway plays died in the first week. You haven't acted in theatre for two years. You're living in the past, lady.

GEORGE:

Okay, take it easy. Let's just solve the problem and get back to work. We're running behind.   *to PATRICK*
What is it about the kiss you don't believe?

PATRICK:

First of all, the primal hairs my gnto. He reouclts the fact
we're living together, and here she is kissing me after
I've just insulted him. Not only is it unbelievable, it's
maudlin

JESSICA:

It's not maudlin, it's tender. And perfectly in character.

PATRICK:

Well, it's not in character for me to let you. At that
moment Frank doesn't want to be touched. It makes his
skin crawl.

JESSICA:

We all make sacrifices, don't we? Personally, I would
rather kiss a monkey's ass. Now let's get on with it.

GEORGE:

Yes, we're wasting time. Maybe there's another way to
make the same point.   *He looks out at ROBERT.*
What do you think, Robert?

ROBERT:

I don't see the problem. I think it works.

PATRICK:

How predictable.

ROBERT:

It's worked all along, hasn't it? Why does it suddenly
not work?

PATRICK:

Why? Because I've never questioned it before. I've
always done it because those were the stage directions.
Your stage directions.

ROBERT:
 I see.

PATRICK:
 That's Phil's line. It's been cut.

ROBERT:
 Why're you so hostile? What did I do?

 He starts down the aisle.

PATRICK:
 I criticize his masterpiece, and suddenly I'm hostile.

ROBERT:
 That's not what I meant, and you know it. If you've
 got a beef, tell me.

GEORGE: *to ROBERT*
 Okay, don't get hot under the collar.   *to PATRICK*
 Let's just cut the kiss and get on with it.   *to JESSICA*
 Put your hand on his shoulder. That'll make the same
 point.

ROBERT: *stepping onstage*
 No, goddamnit!

GEORGE:
 Look, Robert—

ROBERT: *cutting in*
 What the hell is this? That's a very significant and
 subtle moment. She's letting Eric know if it comes to a
 choice she'll choose Frank over him and the son. That's
 what the kiss means.

PATRICK: *to GEORGE*
 Look, mate, get him out of here. He's done his work,
 now let the actors do theirs. We have enough on our
 hands without him on our backs.

JESSICA:
He's not on your back.

PATRICK: *in a rage*
He's here every goddamn day, isn't he? I wouldn't mind if he cringed in a corner somewhere. But no, he paces around like a condemned man. Even when I can't see him, I can *feel* him. He's out there wringing his hands, sighing and wincing, leaping to his feet every time we drop a monosyllable, every time we change a bit of business. Christ, what's more important, George? That we observe every arbitrary stage direction or nail down a character?

GEORGE:
He has a point, Robert.

JESSICA:
George!

PATRICK:
And on top of that, he has the bloody nerve to tell me I'm incompetent.

ROBERT:
I never once said that.

PATRICK:
One hit play to his name, and he thinks he's hot stuff. A play that I helped create, by the way. And I've got the reviews to prove it.

ROBERT:
I never said you were incompetent.

PATRICK:
Maybe I've never played Washington or Dallas or New York, but I've been from one end of this country to the other.

JESSICA:
So has the railroad. Get to the point.

PATRICK: *to ROBERT*
I've done it all, too, from the Greeks to Beckett. I even
had the misfortune to be in two one-acters called *Lay of
the Land* and *Giving Head*. But not even the author of
those two epics had the audacity to walk into a theatre,
as you did today, and say to me, "Are you getting any
better?" She had a little more class than that.

ROBERT:
So that's it.

PATRICK:
And don't try to wriggle out of it.

ROBERT:
That was a joke. You ought to know me better than
that. That's just my sense of humour.

PATRICK:
Sense of humour? Mate, if that's your idea of a joke,
don't ever attempt comedy.

ROBERT:
I was being ironic. I thought you knew that.

PATRICK:
Try flattery next time. Irony belongs in plays. Irony
makes me insecure. Irony makes me think you don't like
what I'm doing.

ROBERT:
Nothing could be further from the truth. I think you're
a superb actor. One of the best actors I've worked with.

PATRICK:
He calls that flattery. He's done two plays and the first
had a cast of two, including myself.

JESSICA: *exasperated*
    Guyrt, what you have things under control let me
    know. I'll be in the dressing-room.

>   *She exits backstage.*

PATRICK: *to ROBERT*
    In the future, if you have a future, don't come bouncing
    into rehearsal and slap an actor on the back and get
    cute. Just tell him he's fantastic and bite your tongue.

ROBERT:
    Go to hell!

NICK: *over the PA*
    George, I realize how little respect you have for stage
    managers, but I feel I have the right to know what's
    going on. Are we having a run-through or just a
    rehearsal? And either way, could we please carry on?

GEORGE:
    Oh, get off my back!

NICK:
    Fine. I only hope you realize that after six-thirty we'll be
    into overtime.

GEORGE:
    I could replace you with a recorded announcement.

NICK:
    At the rate you pay, you just might have to.

PHIL:
    Friends, I've been patient up to now. I've stood here
    and not said a word. Now I'm annoyed. No, incensed.
    Outraged that one member of this company is allowed
    to waste valuable time with his petty, childish behaviour.
    Not only that, he doesn't get reprimanded.

PATRICK:
And who might that be, may I ask?

GEORGE: *angrily*
Okay, okay, this's getting out of hand.

PHIL: *to PATRICK*
If the shoe fits, old buddy. If the shoe fits.

PATRICK:
Well, at least we know he's not talking about himself.

GEORGE:
Goddamnit, let's stop it!   *to the control booth*   Nick,
let's take it from the top. As soon as you're ready.

NICK: *over the PA*
This is a recorded announcement. Places for the top of
Act One. Stand by to go in three minutes. Peggy, could
you come out and put the coffee back in the pot? And
reset the chairs.

PEGGY enters and does her job.

PATRICK: *to PHIL*
That was quite a speech. More than twenty words in a
row and you never dried once. 'Course it was off the
cuff, wasn't it?

He smiles and exits backstage.

PHIL: *to GEORGE*
Did you hear that? He wants to undermine my
confidence. Well, he doesn't know it yet but the laugh's
on him. I don't have any!

He exits backstage.

GEORGE:

Robert, I could've handled him, if you'd just let him. Next time stay out of it.

ROBERT:

Like hell I will. He's not pushing me around. And I'm not losing that moment.

GEORGE:

Stop worrying. I'll have that moment back before we open. I promise.   *ROBERT doesn't seem convinced.*   I give you my word. Trust me.

ROBERT:

George, don't say "Trust me." Any time I hear "Trust me" I know I'm about to be screwed.

GEORGE:

What're you saying? That you don't trust me? That hurts, Robert.

ROBERT:

Listen, you know how long it took me to write *The Care and Treatment of Roses*. I never thought I'd finish.

GEORGE:

You had a big success with your first play. That made the second that much harder to write.

ROBERT:

So what if it gets panned? What'll I have to show for three years of my life? What?

GEORGE:

It won't get panned.

ROBERT:

No?

GEORGE:
It's a beautiful play.

ROBERT:
Yeah, I know. Every play's a beautiful play. Then it
gets knocked, and suddenly everyone has second
thoughts. Instant hindsight.

NICK: *over the PA*
Two minutes to curtain.

GEORGE:
I'm doing my best, okay? I want this to be bigger than
Murphy's Diamond. Robert, this theatre's done four
turkeys in a row. We need a hit or else.

ROBERT:
George, they're waiting to see the whites of my eyes.
I know it.

GEORGE:
Forget I said that, will you?

ROBERT:
No, it's true. They hate success in this country. They
punish you for it. I mean, if I get slaughtered I want it
to be my own fault. They don't know an actor wouldn't
do a moment. He's not the one they'll blame.

GEORGE:
All right, if I don't get you that moment back, I'll call
every critic in town and let them know.

NICK: *over the PA*
One minute to curtain. Clear the stage, please.

GEORGE: *leading ROBERT to the edge of the stage*
Look, do me a favour. Go away. Go to a movie.

ROBERT:
> I hate movies.

GEORGE:
> Then get drunk.

ROBERT:
> I can't drink. I'm not supposed to.

GEORGE:
> Go home then. Take a Valium and sleep until the preview.

ROBERT:
> I already took two Libriums. That's why I'm not supposed to drink. What're you trying to say, George? You don't want me around?

GEORGE:
> I don't think it's wise, do you? For the sake of the play, Robert. The *play*.

ROBERT:
> Okay, I'll go... *He steps off the stage.* But only because you asked me, not because of Flanagan. *He starts up the aisle.* Boy, some day I'd like to get that bastard in an alley... *He smashes his right fist into his palm.*

GEORGE:
> Robert.

ROBERT:
> What?

GEORGE:
> Take another Librium, it wouldn't hurt. Or better still, work on your new play.

The stage lights are dimming and the music has begun.

ROBERT

Jesus, what a business. When you're unknown and fall on your face, they pity you. When you're successful and take a beating, they say you deserved it.

GEORGE:

Forget the critics, will you?

ROBERT:

Who's talking about critics? I meant my writer friends. They're far more vicious.

He exits.

GEORGE steps off the stage and takes his seat on the aisle. The theatre is now in blackness.

GEORGE:

Stay on book, Susi, but forget what I said before. At this stage of the game, harping on lines would only demoralize them more.

Lights up onstage. JESSICA is alone onstage, watering the hanging plants. After a moment, PATRICK comes down the stairs. He is shirtless, and is doing up his belt. He glances at JESSICA, who ignores him. He crosses to the table and pours himself a cup of coffee.

PATRICK: *with an Italian accent*
Why'd you get so upset for, Lizzie? All I asked is how long is he going to stay?

JESSICA:

He's home for the holidays. That's all I know. What do you want me to do, tell him to go to a hotel? He's my son.

66

PATRICK:
I don't like the way he looks at me. Like I'm not good enough to sit on the furniture. He'd better not start that today, because if he does, he'll wish like hell he didn't.

JESSICA:
I don't want trouble, Frank.

PATRICK: *sitting at the table*
Then put his nose back in joint or I'll do it for him.

Slight pause.

JESSICA:
Did you hear the doorbell?

GEORGE leaps to his feet and glares at the control booth, jabbing his finger in the direction of the front door. Suddenly there is a knocking on the door. GEORGE sits and shakes his head.

JESSICA:
That's Eric, now.

She sets down the watering-can and switches off the hi-fi.

PATRICK:
Where the hell are my shoes?

JESSICA:
Honestly, you're worse than Jimmy.   *She stands behind his chair and strokes his chest.*   Your shoes are upstairs. And would you please put on a shirt?

PATRICK:
Lizzie, I'll give the kid two weeks. Either he's gone or I go. Make up your mind.

He rises.

JESSICA:
>   Don't threaten me.

PATRICK:
>   Two weeks, Lissie.

>   *He exits upstairs.*

>   *A second knock on the door. JESSICA crosses into the hallway out of sight. We hear the door open and close.*

PHIL: *off*
>   Hello, Elizabeth.

JESSICA: *off*
>   Hi, Eric. Come in. You look half-frozen.

PHIL: *as he enters*
>   Not half as frozen as that doorbell.

NICK: *over the PA*
>   Sorry.

JESSICA:
>   Here. Let me take your coat.   *She hangs his hat, coat, and scarf on the hat rack.*   I appreciate this, Eric. I wouldn't have called if it wasn't important.

PHIL:
>   I know that. That's why I'm here.   *He crosses near the sofa.*   What is it? Jimmy?

JESSICA:
>   No, it's—Yes, it *is* Jimmy, as a matter of fact.

PHIL:
>   Oh.

JESSICA:

Sit down. I just made a fresh pot of coffee. Have you eaten?

PHIL:

Nothing for me. I just had a snack at the rectory....What's happened, Sis?

JESSICA:

He's quit school.

PHIL:

Jimmy quit school?

He sits on the sofa, far from the arm.

JESSICA:

He says he's had all he can take of university and wants to stay here until he figures out what he wants to do. *She sits on the arm of the sofa.* I'd hate to see him make a mistake, Eric. I don't want him to do something he'll regret later on.

PHIL:

Well, maybe university isn't what he needs right now.

JESSICA: *in order to put her hand on his knee, she has to lean and stretch*

Please, I want you to talk to him. You're the only one who can. He won't listen to me.

PHIL: *sidling over*

And how's Frank feel about all this?

JESSICA:

He doesn't know yet. All he knows is Jimmy's home for the winter break.

PATRICK comes down the stairs, laughing.

PHIL:
   I see.

   PATRICK's laughter stops, then starts again.

PHIL: *rising*
   Hello, Frank.

PATRICK:
   I see. I see, I see, I see...   *to JESSICA*   Well, you
   ought to *see* that kid of yours. He can't even get his socks
   on. What, they don't teach him to drink in
   college?   *to PHIL*   So, Father, I see you. How's it
   going? You still dipping into the poorbox?

JESSICA:
   Frank, you're awful.   *to PHIL*   He's just pulling
   your leg.

PHIL:
   I see!

PATRICK:
   Did she tell you? The kid took a swing at me last night.

PHIL: *putting a cigarette in his mouth*
   No, Elizabeth never mentioned it...

   He fishes in his pockets for matches.

PATRICK:
   He thought he could drink me under the table.

   *He brings out his lighter to light PHIL's cigarette. PHIL
   bends to accept the light, and as he does so, a tall flame
   shoots up like a blowtorch from the adjustable lighter.
   PHIL recoils instinctively. He reaches for the vase of red
   roses on the coffee table and hurls the roses and water into
   PATRICK's face. PHIL dashes around the table, and*

with a wild look of outrage, PATRICK starts after him.
GEORGE rushes down the aisle to the stage. Pandemonium
ensues

GEORGE:
Cut! Cut! Cut!

Blackout.

Music.

Act Two

The dressing-room, four days later. It is 7:45 on opening
night. The dressing-room contains a make-up table with
mirror and four chairs, a clothes-rack, and all the usual
odds and ends. On the table in front of PATRICK's chair
are a shoebox and an electric razor.

Downstage are two chairs separated by a small wooden
stand. On the stand are a newspaper and an ashtray.

Stage right is the washroom. Upstage is the door that leads
into the backstage area. Next to the dressing-room, stage
left, is the Green Room. It is small and contains a fridge,
sofa, end table, a telephone, and a coffee percolator on a
small table. A door leads into the Green Room from the
street.

At rise, JESSICA is dressed in costume, except for her wig
which is still on the wig-stand. She stands near the make-
up table, buttoning her blouse. Then she crosses and looks
at herself in the mirror on the washroom door.

In the Green Room, PATRICK reclines on the sofa,
wearing glasses to read his script. He is dressed in bathrobe
and pants. He glances at his silver pocket watch and goes
back to the script.

PEGGY enters from the street door, carrying a stack of
styrofoam cups, a box of sugar cubes, and a pair of pants
on a wooden hanger. She sets down the cups and the sugar,
then enters the dressing-room and hangs up the pants.

PATRICK:
Any sign of the others?

PEGGY:
Not yet, Pat.

PATRICK:
What about George?

PEGGY:
He still hasn't come back from dinner. I told Susi you
wanted to see him.

She comes back into the Green Room and pours herself a
cup of coffee.

PATRICK watches her a moment.

PATRICK:
God, you're lovely, Peg. A Yeats poem made flesh. Did
I try to get fresh last night?

PEGGY:
Not at all.

PATRICK:
I've drawn a blank, you know.

PEGGY:
You were a perfect gentleman.

73

JESSICA: *into the mirror*
Watch him, Peg.

PATRICK:
I was very fond of a girl once who looked like you.

PEGGY:
I know. You told me last night.

PATRICK:
I did?

PEGGY:
You said I reminded you of your ex-wife. I thought that was very sweet.

PATRICK:
What actually happened after we got back to my place?

PEGGY:
You want the truth?

PATRICK:
Not if you put it like that.

PEGGY: *entering the dressing-room*
It's just that I've never put a man's teeth in a glass before.

PATRICK:
Was it you who did that? Good God.

PEGGY:
I had to. You were so drunk you might've choked in your sleep.

She gets the box with the actors' valuables in it.

PATRICK:

Do you know how hard I searched this morning? I tore the house apart. For God's sake, girl, don't you know you never put teeth in a fridge?

JESSICA: *to PEGGY*

Darling, you just made my day.

PATRICK:

Listen, you two, don't spread that around. You know how malicious the gossip is in this town. "Reputation," Peggy, "is an idle and most false imposition; oft got without merit, and lost without deserving."

JESSICA: *as she returns to the make-up table and sits*

That wasn't from the Scottish play, I hope.

PATRICK:

Othello. And I'm not in the least superstitious.

He removes his glasses, rises, and wanders into the dressing-room, aimless, restless, distracted.

PEGGY smiles, blows him a kiss, then exits into the backstage area.

JESSICA: *after a moment*

It must be late...

PATRICK:

Quarter to eight.

He takes his shirt off the hanger, examines it, then takes a needle and thread from his shoebox. He sits and sews the shirt, singing a few lines from an Irish folk song.

Must be an easier way to make a living.

JESSICA ignores him. She is flattening out her hair with bobby pins in preparation for the wig.

75

PATRICK:

You know, the day I left Ireland was the day after I got
married. The old man called me a lazy, shiftless
sonofabitch and said I'd never do an honest day's work in
my life. Imagine that.

JESSICA:

How prophetic.

PATRICK:

I know, and I wasn't even an actor yet.

JESSICA turns and looks at him.

JESSICA:

How do you feel?

PATRICK:

Why do you ask?

JESSICA:

In case you haven't noticed, you only shaved on one
side of your face.

PATRICK:

Did I?   *He looks in the mirror.*   So I did.

JESSICA:

Your good side, naturally.

PATRICK:

Instinct.   *He leans closer to the mirror.*
Jesus H. Christ...

JESSICA:

What is it?

PATRICK:

The lines around the eyes. Laugh lines. No, they are.
And speaking of laugh lines, I wish I had a few more in
this friggin' play.

He shaves.

JESSICA:
Tell me, Flanagan. Will you go to New York if Bernie
wants you?

PATRICK: *clicking off the razor*
Why wouldn't he want me?

JESSICA:
Oh, I'm sure he will....The cast works so well together.
Not a single weak link. Don't you agree?

PATRICK clicks on his razor and goes back to shaving.

JESSICA:
Why? Who do you think's the weak one? Phil? Tommy?
...Well, that just leaves the two of us, doesn't it?

She turns and goes back to fixing her hair.

PATRICK:
Between you and me, I think we should leave well
enough alone. I think Broadway's had enough domestic
dramas.

JESSICA:
I don't believe you can second-guess an audience any
more than you can the critics. All you can do is a play
you believe in.

PATRICK:
The critics there would laugh us out of town.

JESSICA:
They could do the same here, couldn't they?

PATRICK:
New York's tougher.

JESSICA:

That's never stopped anyone. We take risks all the time,
don't we? New York's just a larger arena. Higher
stakes.

PATRICK:

Well, I'm a Catholic and Catholics are against suicide.
Besides, I don't think we should judge success by New
York. No, really. I've never felt that or I'd be there,
wouldn't I?

JESSICA:

Flanagan, haven't you ever imagined yourself on
Broadway? Believe me, it's the most exciting feeling in
the world, bar none. And you know what's the nicest
part? You feel you deserve it.

PATRICK:

Yes, but how does it feel to get clobbered?

JESSICA:

I wouldn't know.

PATRICK:

You were in two flops.

JESSICA:

The plays were; *I* wasn't.

PATRICK:

Well, I'd feel I deserved it.

JESSICA: *into the mirror*

Our sense of ourselves is so tentative, isn't it? Maybe
that's the real risk we take.

PATRICK:

What's that?

JESSICA:

Facing our own sense of failure

PATRICK:

Look, I make a damn good living here. I have my pick
of roles. I might not be a Star, but who is in this
country? And not everyone feels that compulsion to
outshine.

JESSICA:

You don't need to get defensive. If you don't want to
go, that's your problem.

PATRICK:

Christ, you sound like my ex-wife. All she ever wanted
was Success with a capital S. The old Bitch-Goddess, to
quote William James. As if there's something wrong
with not wanting to work your butt off for agents and
accountants and Internal Revenue.

JESSICA:

Maybe she thought you were settling for too little.

PATRICK:

Well, I've seen the Bitch-Goddess up close. I've had a
sniff or two up her skirt, I know what she's like, she's
insatiable, a parasite, a cancer. She gets on your back
like the Old Man of the Sea and won't get off.

JESSICA:

The trick is to ride success and not let it ride you.

PATRICK:

Well, I'm the one who has to go out there and be good.
She never understood that, my wife. She... *Then, as
if he has said too much already* Look, let's drop it, shall
we? And before I forget: I don't appreciate being
upstaged. You did it again last night.

79

He enters the Green Room and pours himself a coffee.

BECCY *continued*

JESSICA.
When?

PATRICK:
You know when.

JESSICA:
I haven't the foggiest.

PATRICK:
The supper scene.

JESSICA:
Oh, is that why you looked so upset? I thought you had
gas.

PATRICK:
And while we're at it, don't cross your legs onstage.
Last night you sat on the sofa working your legs like a
pair of scissors. Freud would have had a field-day with
that gesture.

JESSICA:
I was simply working up a breeze. Didn't you find it
stifling out there?

PATRICK:
The first three rows don't have to know you're wearing
black lace panties.

JESSICA:
I bet you were the only one who noticed. Did you also
notice the bruise on my left thigh?

PATRICK:

No, I didn't. And it was your right thigh. God knows how you got that.

Enter NICK from the street door.

NICK:

Peggy, have you finished your preset? I want to open the house.

PEGGY:

Nick, that was done ages ago.

NICK:

How about Patrick? Does he have his new prop?

PATRICK:

I do, and I bloody well resent the implication.   *He removes a small Ronson lighter from his pocket and flicks it to produce a small, weak flame.*   To cover myself I should have two of these. If they both fail, I can rub them together to get a light.   *to PEGGY*   That reminds me, love. Could you please put a little more tea in the whiskey bottle? There's only one thing worse than having to drink that vile stuff and that's not having enough. Last night I had to squeeze the bottle.

JESSICA:

I thought he was being cheap with his shots.

NICK:

Oh, and before I forget. Jessica, you still haven't signed the callboard. Some stage managers don't mind, but I'm very, very strict about that.

JESSICA:

You can see I'm here. Sign it yourself.

81

NICK:

I'd rather you did. I don't want to start getting into bad habits. *to PEGGY* What about the cue light? Phil was late last night on his second entrance.

PEGGY:

There's nothing wrong with the cue light. He's been taking a verbal cue from Pat and he missed it.

PATRICK:

He was too busy giving himself the last rites.

NICK: *to PEGGY*

Well, tell him I'll cue him in. I don't want that to happen again.

PEGGY:

I'll remind him.

She exits into the backstage area.

NICK starts into the Green Room. He stops suddenly and turns.

NICK:

Now, Jessica, please.

He exits out the street door.

JESSICA:

Did you hear that? Who does he think he's ordering around?

PATRICK:

What do you expect, reverence? I find him refreshingly democratic. He treats us all with equal contempt.

GEORGE enters from the backstage area. Dressed in a navy-blue suit, he carries a bouquet of long-stemmed red roses and a shopping bag containing wine and presents.

GEORGE:
Hello, Jess, Patrick.

JESSICA:
Oh, George, am I glad to see you.   *as GEORGE sets*
down the shopping bag and returns to her   Don't you look
handsome.

GEORGE:
You look wonderful yourself, love.   *He kisses her*
cheek.   Radiant.   *He hands JESSICA the flowers.*
These are for you, Jess. I hope you like roses.

JESSICA:
I adore roses. Oh, aren't they lovely.   *She embraces*
him.   Thank you, darling.   *She kisses his cheek.*

PATRICK: *into his newspaper*
What's in the bag, a vase?

GEORGE:
Oh, God. I completely forgot.

JESSICA:
That's okay. I'll find one.

GEORGE:
Stay where you are. I'll get one in Props.

JESSICA:
No, I insist. Besides, I have to sign the callboard or
Nick'll report me to Equity.

She exits out the street door.

PATRICK: *to himself*
Roses. How cliché.

GEORGE takes a box tied with ribbons from the shopping
bag and crosses to PATRICK.

GEORGE:
For you, Pat.

PATRICK:
For me? You're kidding.

> *GEORGE tosses him the box, and PATRICK flicks off the ribbon and lifts the lid. He laughs.*

GEORGE:
You recognize it?

PATRICK: *removing a catcher's mask*
The catcher's mask from *Murphy's Diamond*. Thanks, mate, I'm touched. No, really. That play meant a lot to me. When it closed, there was more of a hole in my life than when I got divorced. Then again, I had more fun in the play.   *He puts the mask back in the box and puts the box on the stand.*   Did Susi give you my message?

GEORGE: *taking two bottles of champagne from the shopping bag and crossing to the fridge*
Yeah, what is it? She said it was urgent.

PATRICK:
It's crucial. Did you speak to Phil about last night?

GEORGE:
Yeah, I did. And believe me, he's upset enough already.

PATRICK:
He ought to be. He botched the entire first act.

GEORGE:
Look, it wasn't that serious. The audience didn't even notice.

PATRICK:

How could they help but notice? There we are, our big scene at the breakfast table. He's right in the middle of his long speech and suddenly he gets this strange look in his eye. "Excuse me, Frank," he says, and walks offstage.

GEORGE:

He dried. He ran back to get his line from Peggy.

PATRICK:

I know, and left me alone on stage. No dialogue, no business, nothing to do but sit there and eat my bacon and eggs. He was gone so long I had a second cup of coffee.

GEORGE:

It didn't seem that long. I'm telling you, no one noticed.

PATRICK:

George, you've never been an actor. Long doesn't begin to describe it. Now I know what they mean by a pregnant pause. By the time he came back I was in labour. And then he sits back down as though nothing has happened and says, "So as I was saying, Frank..."

GEORGE:

Pat, it won't happen again. Next time he'll just ad lib.

PATRICK:

Next time?

GEORGE:

If it does happen, I mean.

PATRICK:

There better not be a next time, mate. Because if he walks offstage tonight, I'm walking off behind him. And I don't care if Feldman *is* in the audience.

85

GEORGE:
Forget Feldman. I wish I'd never heard of Feldman. He's probably so jaded he won't like the show anyway.

PATRICK:
That's what Jess thinks.

GEORGE:
What do you mean?

PATRICK:
She's heard he's had second thoughts about the play. That's between you and me.

GEORGE:
That's ridiculous. Feldman's crazy about it. Why do you think he's coming tonight?

PATRICK:
If you ask me, she's getting cold feet. Oh, she puts up a good front, but underneath it all she's terrified. I think she's into the sauce.

GEORGE:
You think so?

PATRICK:
I know so. It's those New York critics. She's convinced they're out to get her.

GEORGE:
The thing to remember, Patrick, is no actor is under any obligation to this show after it closes here. That goes for Jess or anyone. Even you.

PATRICK:
Oh, I couldn't go if I wanted to. Didn't I tell you? I'm already committed to another play.

Enter JESSICA carrying a vase.

JESSICA:
No sign of Phil or Tommy? It's almost eight.

GEORGE.
They may be in the theatre. I'll check with front-of-house.

> *JESSICA carries the vase and roses into the washroom, leaving the door ajar. She runs the water. GEORGE closes the door quickly and takes PATRICK aside.*

GEORGE:
What do you mean you can't do the play? That's not what you told me six weeks ago.

PATRICK:
Sorry mate, you misunderstood.

GEORGE:
You knew the whole production might move to New York. I made that clear.

PATRICK:
I already gave my word. The director's an old, old friend of mine. I can't let him down.

GEORGE:
Who is it?

PATRICK:
I'm not in a position to say at the moment. Just a dear, dear friend.

GEORGE:
What play are you doing?

PATRICK:
What's that matter? The point is I have a commitment which I don't intend to break. I gave my word, and that's it.

GEORGE:

> Well, the most important thing right now is that we do the play here and do it right. I don't care what happens after that.

He starts for the backstage door.

PATRICK:

> George.

GEORGE stops.

> I'm sorry.

GEORGE:

> It's okay, Pat. I understand.

PATRICK:

> And speak to Mastorakis again, will you? By now he's probably forgotten.

GEORGE:

> Relax. Stop worrying. Just go out there tonight and have fun.

He exits into the backstage area.

PATRICK:

> Relax, he says. That's easy for him to say. His work's done. He can sit in the dark now and chew his cuticles. I've got to go out there with a kid fresh out of Theatre School and a forty-four-year-old Greek with a mind like Rip Van Winkle.

The doorknob rattles.

JESSICA: *off*

> This damn door's stuck again. Give us a pull, Flanagan.

PATRICK:
    One second.

        He removes a bottle of whiskey from the shoebox on the
        make up table and takes a good drink.

JESSICA: *off*
    Flanagan!

PATRICK:
    Hold your horses.

NICK: *over the PA, as PATRICK crosses to the washroom*
    Good evening, ladies and gentlemen, this is your half-
    hour call. If you are in the theatre and have not signed
    the callboard, would you please do so now?

        PATRICK pulls the door open. JESSICA strides out.

JESSICA:
    If he mentions that friggin' callboard one more time, I'll
    ram it up his nose.

        She sets the vase on the table and arranges the roses.

        SUSI enters from the backstage area with telegrams.

SUSI:
    Telegrams for Jessica. And Patrick. And for Tom and
    Phil.

PATRICK:
    Did you say *for* Tom and Phil? Or *from* Tom and
    Phil?   *He rips open a telegram and scans it.*   ''Best
    luck with *Roses*. Break your legs. Edna.''

SUSI:
    Shouldn't that be ''break a leg''?

89

PATRICK:
Not if you knew my ex-wife. She's very precise.

JESSICA:
This one's from Innerkip. "Knock 'em dead." Signed "Percy."

SUSI:
Who's Percy?

JESSICA:
I haven't the foggiest. Where the hell is Innerkip?

PATRICK:
Never mind Innerkip. Where the hell is Tom and Phil?

GEORGE enters from the backstage area.

GEORGE:
Susi, Nick's looking for you. He wants to open the house.

SUSI:
He's gotta be kidding. It's like a sauna in there.

GEORGE:
Speak to him. That's between the two of you....Can I see you a moment, love? The Green Room...
to PATRICK and JESSICA   I'll be right back.

He guides SUSI into the Green Room. PATRICK and JESSICA continue to read their telegrams.

SUSI:
I know. Keep my voice down.

GEORGE:
I don't want them to know I'm worried. Nick's trying to locate the others. Did Tom say what he was doing today?

SUSI:

How should I know?

GEORGE·

I thought he was at your place last night.

SUSI:

George, give me a break. I know Phil was shooting a film this afternoon. Some industrial film.

GEORGE:

Where?

SUSI:

In the garment district, I think.

GEORGE:

Would his girl-friend know?

SUSI:

Gloria? She might. His mother would know for sure. He has to call in once a day or she phones Missing Persons.

GEORGE:

You have her number?

SUSI:

She's in the lobby.

GEORGE:

Great. Ask her where he's working and have Nick call them.

SUSI:

Right.   *She starts out, then turns.*   What about Feldman? Should I bring him back as soon as he picks up his tickets?

GEORGE:

No, keep him out. I don't want him around Patrick.
Where's Robert?

He sits on the sofa.

SUSI:

Where he always watches the show. From the booth.

GEORGE:

Well, tell him to get his ass down here on the double.
The least he can do is put in an appearance.

SUSI:

Gotcha.

*She exits. In a rage GEORGE hammers his fists on the
sofa and stamps his feet. PATRICK and JESSICA
exchange a glance.*

GEORGE: *to himself:*

Jesus Christ, tonight of all nights!

*Enter PHIL from the street door. He's out of breath and
visibly upset. He wears sunglasses and a beret. Under his
arm is a much-worn copy of the script.*

PHIL:

Forgive me, people. I apologize. It's inexcusable.
George, old buddy, don't look at me like that. I'm not
to blame. I swear to God.

He puts down his script and kicks off his shoes.

GEORGE:

Where've you been?

PHIL: *as he crosses to the clothes-rack and removes his shirt*
They ran overtime. They knew I had an opening tonight, and they still lied about the time. I will never buy my mother another Singer sewing machine. Oh, George, do you know if Gloria's picked up her ticket?

GEORGE:
She's in the audience.

PHIL:
I wasn't sure she'd come.

JESSICA:
Don't tell me you two are still fighting.

PHIL:
Can you blame us? Every time we discuss marriage my mother goes to bed and refuses to eat.

He removes his pants. He's wearing a pair of bright red bikini briefs.

PATRICK:
Well, look at *her*. Red bikinis. Very, very smart, love. A gift from Mother? Or a pair of Mother's?

PHIL: *putting on the priest's pants*
I always wear red opening night. I feel like a bullfighter. It's gore or be gored.

PHIL removes his sunglasses. He leans forward to examine his left eye in the mirror. JESSICA glances his way, does a double-take, then stares.

JESSICA:
Oh, my God, he's got a black eye.

PHIL:
It's nothing, nothing.

GEORGE:

Let me see.   *He inspects the eye.*   Phil, how did you

do that?

PHIL:

I can't tell you. I'm too ashamed. Please, I'm okay.
Don't be alarmed.

JESSICA:

I'll get some ice.

GEORGE:

Forget the ice. There isn't time. Phil, you'll have to hide
it with make-up. How's your vision?

PHIL:

Twenty-twenty, old buddy. I just can't feel my
cheekbone. But compared to my hand, George. My
hand.

GEORGE:

What's wrong with your hand?

PATRICK:

He's been hitting himself again. I told you to stop doing
that.

PHIL:

Just what I'd expect from you. I'm in exquisite pain,
and he laughs.

GEORGE:

Let's see.

PHIL holds out his hand.

Looks fine to me.

PHIL:
I think it's broken. The index finger. Look: blue. A
hairline fracture, at least. Oh, God. God. Why tonight?

He continues getting dressed

GEORGE:
So what happened?

PHIL:
Incredible, huh? Phil Mastorakis. I abhor violence. I'm
squeamish. That dumb film. That's what did it. Take
after take after take. And to lie to me, to deceive me
about the time. A rage, George. I was in a rage when I
left. Stormed out. Two blocks later, it happened.

GEORGE:
What happened?

PHIL:
The fight. The fist fight. How do you think I got this
shiner?

GEORGE: *exasperated*
Phil, that's what I'm trying to find out!

PHIL:
These two musclemen, right? They're strolling towards
me. I.Q. tattooed on their biceps. With a penknife. I go
to pass, one points to my beret and says, "Artiste!" I
went berserk, George. I saw red. I ran back and took a
swing at the guy. Next thing I know I'm sitting on the
sidewalk, my beret in my lap, some guy walks by and
drops in a quarter.

He tosses the beret on the make-up table.

JESSICA:
That was a crazy thing to do, Phil. You could've been
killed.

95

PHIL:

>Don't remind me. And you know what's even crazier? For twenty years I've wanted to be called an artist in this country and the first guy who says it I *punch* him.

>*Enter NICK and PEGGY from the street door.*

NICK:

>George, the house is in. I've been calling—Oh, hello, Phil, you're here.   *to GEORGE*   Thanks for letting me know.

JESSICA:

>Obviously you never checked the callboard.   *to PHIL* Did I tell you? Nick is very, very strict about that.

NICK:

>All kidding aside, I haven't been able to reach Tom. Does anyone know where he went today?

PHIL: *shocked*

>He's late?!

NICK:

>Take it easy, Phil. There's no need to panic.

PHIL:

>Fine. Great. Fantastic. We go up in twenty minutes, and there's no need to panic?

GEORGE:

>Nick's right. Maybe he got held up in traffic. *to NICK*   Did you call his new number?

NICK:

>Naturally I called his new number. There was no answer. If I'd called his new number and spoken to him, I wouldn't be here now asking the cast if anyone knew where he was, would I?

GEORGE:
Listen, you pompous ass...

PHIL: *cutting in*
I think he mentioned a wedding. Yeah, he did. He had a wedding to go to.

JESSICA:
A wedding?

PHIL:
His father was getting married again. That's why he came to a preview.

NICK:
What church? Do you know?

PHIL:
Wasn't in a church. He was getting married in his back yard. Weather permitting.

NICK:
Do you know where he lives?

PHIL:
Let's see. I wasn't paying that much attention.... No, I'm sorry. I can't... I can't...   *He shrugs.*

PATRICK:
The word is remember.

PHIL:
Hey, look, Flanagan...

JESSICA: *cutting in*
Phil, it might help if we knew his father's name. Did Tom ever menton it?

PHIL:

His first name, huh? Let's see. I'm lousy with names. God, it's right on the tip of my tongue.

GEORGE:

Think hard.

PHIL:

Okay, but don't stand over me like that. I have to do this my way.... Tom and I had lunch at Luigi's on Tuesday. He ordered french fries and a cheeseburger with the works...

GEORGE: *cutting in*

We don't care what he ate, just his father's name.

PHIL:

I'm working up to it.... And I ordered an egg salad sandwich on brown and a chocolate milk shake. We'd just got our order and Tom said he had to go to a wedding the afternoon of the opening.

GEORGE:

What did you say?

PHIL:

I said "Who's getting married?"

GEORGE:

And he said?

PHIL:

His old man.

GEORGE: *exasperated*

Phil, we know that!

PHIL:
Only he didn't say his old man They call each other by
their first names. How often do you hear a father and
son…?

GEORGE: *cutting in, grabbing PHIL by the front of his shirt*
The name, Phil! Just the name!

PHIL:
Percy.

JESSICA:
Percy? Oh, my God, Tommy's in Innerkip.

GEORGE:
Innerkip?

JESSICA:
See for yourself.   *She hands him the telegram.*   It
must be his. There must've been a mix-up.

GEORGE:
Where's Innerkip?

JESSICA:
Listen, until a second ago we never knew who Percy
was.

NICK: *taking the telegram*
I'll get on it right away.

> *He enters the Green Room and uses the phone, quietly
> ad-libbing his phone calls.*
>
> *PEGGY, who has been sitting on the sofa, rises and
> wanders into the dressing-room. She and GEORGE
> exchange a worried look.*

JESSICA:
What time is it?

PEGGY:
Exactly 8:12.

JESSICA:
8:12. Almost time for, "Ladies and gentlemen, this is your fifteen minute call." So help me, if his voice comes over that box, I'll throttle him.

> *NICK overhears this remark and makes an obscene gesture. ROBERT, pale and somewhat nervous, enters from the street door, carrying a magnum of champagne. GEORGE notices his entrance and enters the Green Room, putting his finger to his lips to silence him.*

PHIL:
Anyone have a cigarette?

JESSICA:
I thought you quit.

PHIL: *as JESSICA passes him a cigarette*
Seven years ago, but now and then I get the urge. Right now I need a cigarette.

> *NICK hangs up. Looks grimly at GEORGE.*

NICK:
No answer.

GEORGE:
All right then, I want to talk to the two of you, and I don't want hysterics.   *to ROBERT*   Is that understood?

ROBERT:
What is it?

GEORGE:

Tom still hasn't shown up and there's a real possibility that he might not. The question now is what to do.

NICK:

What choice do we have?

GEORGE:

We can't cancel, Nick. There are eighteen members of the press out there. They have openings every night this week. If we cancel, we may not get reviewed till the middle of next week, if then.

NICK:

So?

GEORGE:

Besides, Feldman's out there. We can't assume he'll just cool his heels till tomorrow night. Bernie's a busy man, and for all we know Tom might've been in a serious accident.

ROBERT:

What are you saying, George?

GEORGE:

What I'm saying, Robert, is that I need someone to go on for Tom. Now there are only three people who can do it. You, me, and Nick.

NICK:

Me? I can't do it. I'm running the show.

GEORGE:

Exactly.

ROBERT:

Then I guess it's up to you, George.

GEORGE:

    Robert, you want me to stumble through your beautiful play with a script in my hand? Playing a college student in polo pajamas?

ROBERT:

    George, I am not an actor!

GEORGE:

    You used to be.

ROBERT:

    That was eight years ago, and you know why I quit? Because I was terrified. I made Phil Mastorakis look confident.

GEORGE:

    I heard you were a wonderful actor.

ROBERT:

    Who told you that?

GEORGE:

    Phil. He said you played the juvenile lead in his first TV show, "Six Mangoes to Morocco."

ROBERT:

    George, you can't expect me to just step into the role at a moment's notice. I'm not prepared. I don't even know the lines.

NICK:

    You wrote them, didn't you?

ROBERT:

    That doesn't mean I *know* them.

GEORGE:

    Ad lib what you don't remember.

ROBERT:

Like hell I will. I worked over those words like a blacksmith. It's a tightly-written play. If I left out certain lines, the rest of the play wouldn't make sense.

GEORGE:

Look, that's the best thing we have going for us, the play. The *play*, Robert. It's so strong that even Phil can't screw it up. And if you're worried about being nervous, don't be. Just go out there and *be* nervous. Don't try to hide it. Let it show, and before you know it...

ROBERT: *cutting in*
No!

GEORGE:

There's something else I want to say, and I've never said this before. In some ways you would have been a better choice for this role than Tom.

ROBERT:

Get serious.

GEORGE:

It's true. Tom has to *act* the part, you've lived it. Robert, you *are* Jimmy.

ROBERT:

I'm not. I'm all those characters. I'm Frank and Eric. George, I'm even Elizabeth. Jimmy's just one facet of myself.

GEORGE:

Fine, but right now the facet of yourself that is Jimmy can save the show, if you'll just do it. Don't think of Jess and Phil and all they have invested in tonight. Don't think of me, either: our friendship doesn't matter. Do it for yourself, Robert, because you're the one who's

got the most at stake here. You're the one who'll have
to live with yourself if you chicken out now and let
Feldman go home empty-handed.

ROBERT:
You're a real bastard, George. You know that?

GEORGE: *to NICK*
He'll do it.   *to ROBERT*   Just one word of
advice: look each actor in the eye when you're talking to
him. That's very important.

ROBERT:
If I look Phil in the eye, he'll forget his lines for sure.

GEORGE:
All right. Look them all in the eye except for Phil. With
Phil, look over his shoulder or above his head.

ROBERT:
One more thing: I'm not going on in those stupid polo
pajamas.

GEORGE:
Nick, go up to Wardrobe. Get Robert another pair of
pajamas. Meanwhile, I'll talk to the cast.

NICK:
No problem.

He exits.

*GEORGE gives ROBERT the thumbs-up sign and enters
the dressing-room.*

JESSICA: *as she puts on her wig and turns to GEORGE*
There. How do I look? Don't tell me: ghastly. Cheap
and ghastly.

GEORGE:
    You look gorgeous. It's perfect.

JESSICA.
    Liar. It's horrid, and you know it. I look like a Barbie
    doll for octogenarians.

    She returns to the mirror and begins to comb her wig.

    ROBERT enters the dressing-room.

PATRICK:
    Oh-oh, just what we need: Banquo's ghost.
    to JESSICA, quickly   And I didn't quote the Scottish
    play.

JESSICA:
    No, but you came damn close. Chin up, Robert. This is
    your big night. Peg, be a dear and take that bottle. If
    he holds it any tighter, he'll pop the cork.

PEGGY: *taking the bottle*
    I'll put it in the fridge.

GEORGE:
    One second, Peg. I have something important to say to
    the cast and I want you to hear it. This concerns us all.

PHIL:
    I hope it's about these new shoes you got me, George,
    because they squeak.

JESSICA:
    Is that what that was last night, your shoes? I thought
    we had a loose floorboard.

PHIL: *to GEORGE*

There. You see,

GEORGE:

Phil, I've got more on my mind right now than new shoes. I promise you'll have another pair for tomorrow.

PHIL:

Can't Nick oil them?

PEGGY:

Phil, you don't oil shoes, you oil a hinge. Shoes you wear in.

GEORGE:

All right, let's get down to business.... Now folks, we still haven't been able to locate Tom. I'm sure he'll arrive any second, but just in case...

PHIL:

Incredible. Stalin tracked down Trotsky in Mexico and put an axe in his head and we can't locate one lost actor.

GEORGE:

Look, Phil, I need the full co-operation of every member of the cast. It's very close to curtain, so time is precious. This show, cast, is going on tonight, with or without Tom.

PATRICK:

Really?

JESSICA:

What do you have in mind, George?

> *NICK enters, holding the bottoms of a pair of striped pajamas against himself.*

NICK: *to GEORGE*
How do these look?

JESSICA:
Oh, no! If you think I'm going onstage with that little martinet playing my son, you've got another think coming!

NICK:
These are not for me, they're for him.

JESSICA:
Robert?

PATRICK:
Oh, Jesus.

GEORGE:
Look, either Robert gets ready to go on right now or we cancel tonight's show and kiss Broadway goodbye. It's up to you.

PHIL:
The kid can act, George, I've seen him. He's dynamite!

GEORGE:
Now I've already discussed this with Robert, and he's more than willing to jump into the breach. Aren't you, Robert?   *then*   Aren't you?   *ROBERT nods, sickly.*   Besides, Pat, he's close to the right age and he knows all the lines. In fact, he knows all the parts and all the blocking.

PATRICK:
I know. And he'll stand out there tonight and correct all our grammar. This show could run till morning.

GEORGE:

What's more, I intend to make an announcement. I'll go up on stage and explain that something has happened to the actor playing Jimmy and that tonight the playwright will step in. They'll love it.

PATRICK:

You overestimate their good will.

GEORGE:

Are you kidding? Remember *Murphy's Diamond*? The night the lights went out in the middle of Act One? I walked calmly down the aisle and up on stage and told the audience we were starting over. Remember what they did?

PATRICK:

Distinctly. A mad crush for the exits.

GEORGE:

They cheered is what they did. They felt they were sharing in a crisis. Half of them come here anyway expecting the set to fall on the actors' heads, and when it does, they adore it...

PATRICK:

That's comforting to know, George.

JESSICA:

Well, I, for one, Flanagan, think it's quite courageous of Robert. I certainly wouldn't want to be in his shoes. I think he deserves our full support.

PHIL:

Bravo, Robert!

GEORGE:

Besides, you've all been through a lot worse than this, I'm sure. I know this is difficult, but you're all professionals, and I know you can rise to the occasion and turn this crisis into a triumph.

PHIL:

Hear, hear!

JESSICA:

And let's not forget Bernie. He flew all this way to see a show, so let's give him one. Let's give him the best damn performance he's ever seen!

PHIL:

Three cheers for Robert! Hip, hip, hurrah!

ALL except PATRICK:

Hip, hip, hurrah! Hip, hip—

TOM rushes in, dressed in a suit and tie, the tie loose, the jacket in his hand.

ALL including PATRICK:

Hurrah!!!

TOM:

Oh, Jeez, I'm sorry. Honest. I'm sorry, everybody. Don't be mad.

JESSICA:

Thank God.

TOM:

I know: I'm late. I'll get dressed.

He rushes to the clothes rack and begins to tear off his clothes.

GEORGE:
Slow down, Tom. Don't get yourself in a state.

TOM.
My first part, and this happens. I can't think straight.
It's like a nightmare.

He rips off his shirt, popping the buttons.

PHIL:
He thinks *he's* distraught? My whole career just flashed
before my eyes. Can you imagine going onstage with
Robert?

*ROBERT wanders into the Green Room and stretches out
on the sofa.*

NICK: *to TOM*
If it's not too much to ask, where the hell have you
been?

JESSICA:
Never you mind. The thing is he's here and all is
forgiven. Just take those pajamas back to Wardrobe and
sign Tommy in. I wouldn't want you remembering your
precious callboard right in the middle of a sound cue.

NICK exits, glowering.

TOM: *removing his pants*
My Dad got married, George. He would've been hurt, I
hadn't gone. Like I didn't want to go. It's forty miles
outside the city.

JESSICA:
Innerkip?

TOM:
How'd you know?

JESSICA:
Tell you later

TOM: *putting on his pajama top*
The cab had a flat on the way back. I never knew that
cabs got flats. I thought they weren't like other cars.

JESSICA:
Shouldn't it only take a few minutes to fix a tire?

TOM:
Sure, if you got a spare. Like, he had no spare. I mean,
there we were trying to flag down the highway on
another cab. Jeez, you can never get a cab when you
want one. Oh, yeah, I forgot. Like, could someone play
the driver? I'm a little fixed for cash.

PHIL:
Play the driver?

JESSICA:
Fixed for cash?

PEGGY:
I'll take care of it.

GEORGE:
And tell Nick to get back down here. On the double.
Tell him to bring back the pajamas.

PEGGY exits. GEORGE enters the Green Room.

On your feet, Robert. We might need you after all. Tom
is *pissed.*

He re-enters the dressing-room.

PATRICK:
Jesus H. Christ.

He turns away in disgust. PHIL buries his face in his hands.

TOM:
    No, really, I'm fine. Look: I'm fine.

He tries to stand on his head.

GEORGE:
    What'd you have to drink, Tom?

TOM:
    Punch.

PHIL:
    Punch?

TOM:
    Pineapple punch.

GEORGE:
    What was in it?

JESSICA:
    Need you ask? Look at him.

PATRICK:
    He can't go onstage like that, George. He'll fall asleep on the sofa. Stick his head in the sink.

    He rushes into the Green Room, glancing at ROBERT, and pours a coffee. PHIL puts on his scarf and overcoat.

PHIL:
    Wait till my shrink hears about this. And he thinks *he* has problems!

JESSICA: *helping TOM who is struggling to get his pajama bottoms on over his slippers*
    Here we go. One leg at a time. That's it.

TOM:

Know what Percy thinks? He thinks I got drunk because
I blew the hitch he married. That wasn't the reason. I
just didn't know the spike was punched.

JESSICA   *to GEORGE*

And he has to make it through a four-page monologue.

She returns to the make-up table.

TOM:

Jesus H. Christ.

PATRICK: *returning with the coffee*

That's my line, cocky, get your own. Here, drink
this.   *TOM does.*   More. More.... Okay, George,
he's all yours. Just don't drown him.

GEORGE:

Come on, Tom.

He leads TOM into the washroom, leaving the door ajar.

PATRICK:

Just remember, Thomas, no matter how much you ache
to go to the can, don't walk offstage before intermission.
I already had one actor pull that.

PHIL:

Then don't cross your eyes in the middle of my speech.
That's why I dried.

PATRICK:

I never crossed my eyes.

PHIL:

No? What would you call it?

PATRICK:

I might've winced a little.

PHIL.

Winced?

PATRICK:

And no bloody wonder. There was enough garlic on your breath to peel the paint off a Pontiac. How's he doing, George? Is he sober and repentant?

PHIL:

I'm warning you, Flanagan. Don't ever do what you did last night. If you ever call me up again at three a.m.....

PATRICK:

I was sound asleep.

PHIL:

Accusing me of walking offstage just to spite you. Using that filthy gutter language.

PATRICK:

You dreamt it.

PHIL:

I suppose my mother dreamt it, too? She has her own extension. She heard every word.

GEORGE and TOM come out of the washroom, TOM drying his head with a towel. He squirts water from between his teeth.

PATRICK:

I wish I found that amusing.

Enter NICK, with pajamas.

NICK:

How is he? Can he go on?

GEORGE:

I need time to sober him up. Make an announcement.
Tell the audience there's been a delay. Meanwhile, get
Robert into those pajamas. Just in case.

NICK:

We can't hold much past 8:45. Nine at the latest.

GEORGE:

Listen, we'll hold as long as it takes. We're not
cancelling this show unless the actors want to. Is that
understood?

NICK:

Perfectly.

GEORGE:

If I can just get him to the point where he can say,
"The punch is spiked."

TOM: *looking up*
I don't say that, do I?

GEORGE:

Let's take a walk, Tom. Better still, let's jog. On your
mark, Tom. Go.

> *He starts off with TOM trailing behind, the towel draped
> around his neck. They exit.*

PATRICK:

The late-comers are in for a treat. Wait'll they see
George and Tom jogging around the block.

> *Pause.*

115

JESSICA:
   What time is it?

NICK.
   Five minutes to curtain,

JESSICA:
   This is what happens when you don't have understudies.

PHIL:
   Understudies? They're too cheap to hire a prompter.

   *He reacts, turns and sits at the make-up table. Takes his
   script and runs lines.*

   Pause.

PATRICK:
   The intangibility of the stage. A few remembered
   moments that add up to a life. Like pissing into the
   wind.

PHIL:
   God, you're contemptible.

   *NICK enters the Green Room. Tosses the pajamas to
   ROBERT.*

NICK:
   Here. George wants you to get into these and be ready
   to go.

ROBERT:
   Screw off.

NICK:
   I'm not asking you, I'm telling you. George may treat
   you with kid gloves, but right now you're just another
   actor. So get dressed.

ROBERT:
Like hell I will. I'm not wearing these stupid striped pajamas.

NICK:
Suit yourself. Go on in your jock-strap for all I care.

He starts to exit.

ROBERT:
I'm not wearing make-up, either!

NICK:
Wear what you want. I just don't want you upsetting the actors. You get it?

He exits.

JESSICA:
Fascist!

ROBERT enters the dressing-room and hurls the pajamas on the table.

ROBERT:
It's not fair, Jess. Why should I have to go out there tonight and butcher my own play? That's what actors get paid for.

He sits at the make-up table.

JESSICA:
Don't fret, my heart. I worry more when a show goes too smoothly. I've been in Broadway shows that barely made it to curtain.

PATRICK:
I beg to differ. I happened to star in his first play and the only crisis we had was the one he wrote in the second act.

117

PHIL:
> That's not what I heard.

PATRICK:
> Then again, his first work was called a play. This one's being touted as a vehicle. A vehicle for Miss Jessica Logan. From Art to Mechanics at one fell swoop.

JESSICA: *springing to her feet*
> All right, you sonofabitch, *that* was from *Macbeth*.

PATRICK:
> What? "One fell swoop"?

JESSICA:
> Hurry up. Walk backwards out of the room, turn around three times, and beg permission to come in.

PATRICK:
> If I walk out of this room, I won't be coming back.

JESSICA:
> If you have no respect for yourself, at least have some for tradition. Right now we need all the luck we can get. Or don't you want this show to go on?

PATRICK:
> Look, how can we miss? We have a Star in the cast. It's not like *Murphy's Diamond*, is it, Robert? We have a real Star. A Star who can lure Bernie Feldman up to the boondocks.

JESSICA:
> It also helps if the play is good.

PATRICK:
> By the way, I loved your interview in the *Globe*. *He holds up the newspaper.* Isn't it noble of Miss Logan to

act in a ncw play at a two-hundrcd scat thcatrc? No
dressing-room of her own. No star on the door.
Working for scale with local character actors.

PHIL:

Hey, get off her back, why don't you?

PATRICK:

That's from the play, isn't it? Are you talking to me or
just running lines?

PHIL:

I've had it up to here with you and your sick jokes.
This is a real lady here, and that's more than I can say
for you.

JESSICA:

Why don't you save your nastiness for Act One and just
let the rest of us get into character?

PATRICK:

Don't pull rank on me.

JESSICA:

I'm not pulling rank. I'm simply telling you to shut
your mouth. I don't want to hear about Bernie Feldman
or being a Star or anything else you dredge up to cover
your own fear.

PATRICK:

My fear?

JESSICA:

And as for New York, Buster, I wouldn't want you in
the cast anyway. After this show closes here, I'll be quite
happy to read your obituary!

NICK: *over the PA*

Ladies and gentlemen, may I have your attention, please. Due to technical difficulties, the curtain will go up a few minutes late. We're working on it, so please bear with us. Thank you.

ROBERT:

Jess, I feel weird. I'm dizzy. My ears are ringing...

JESSICA:

Quick. Put your head between your knees.

He does.

Phil, get your smelling salts.

PHIL:

Here.

JESSICA:

Sit up, Robert.

He does.

Now breathe in. *She holds the bottle under his nose.* That's it. Again.

ROBERT:

Jess, I think I'm going to be sick...

He bolts up, covers his mouth, and lurches out the street door.

PATRICK:

What was wrong with the washroom? Be just our luck if he brings up all over a critic.

He picks up the shoebox and starts for the washroom.

PHIL:

Get them first. That's what I always say.

JESSICA. *to PATRICK*

Where do you think you're going? Stop him, Phil. He's got a bottle.

PHIL:

A bottle?   *He bounds from his chair and gets between PATRICK and the washroom.*   Okay, old buddy, I'll take that.   *snapping his fingers*   Hand it over.

PATRICK:

Do that again, I'll break your arm. Now get out of my way.

PHIL:

Did you hear that? He threatened the Equity deputy!

JESSICA:

What the hell do you think you're doing, drinking before an opening?   *as PEGGY returns*   Where's Nick? I won't step on that stage tonight if this sonofabitch takes a drink!

> *Enter GEORGE and TOM, both gasping for breath. GEORGE now has the towel draped around his neck. TOM appears to have sobered considerably. He halts at the coffee percolator and pours himself a black coffee.*

GEORGE:

Peggy, what time is it?

PEGGY:

8:40.

> *PATRICK replaces the shoebox on the make-up table. GEORGE puts on PEGGY's headset which is on the wall in the Green Room.*

GEORGE:

>Nick, are you in the booth?... Okay, we can go any time you're ready. Is Robert there?   Tell him to relax. Tell him we won't be needing him.... Yeah, Tom's much better, he'll be fine...

>*He replaces the headset.*

>*TOM exiles himself in the Green Room and stares at the floor.*

NICK: *over the PA*

>Okay, cast, we'll be starting in exactly five minutes. So stand by beginners for Act One. Have a good show.

>*PATRICK, JESSICA and PHIL each sit and give last minute attention to themselves in the mirror. GEORGE crosses to JESSICA.*

GEORGE: *kissing her cheek*

>Good show, love. I'll see you later.

JESSICA:

>Are you watching the show?

GEORGE:

>No, I'll be in the lobby.

JESSICA:

>Would you have your wife sit near the front?

GEORGE:

>Why?

JESSICA:

>I want to know if she can see up my skirt. Tell her to sneeze once for yes.

>*GEORGE crosses to PATRICK who is running a lint brush over his pants.*

GEORGE:
What can I say, Pat?

PATRICK.
A simple "Thank you" would suffice. "You're a helluva great actor" would be even better.

GEORGE:
How about both?

PATRICK:
Terrific, mate. Only next time think of it yourself.

GEORGE moves to PHIL.

GEORGE:
Phil.

PHIL: *staring into the mirror*
Oh, gentle Jesus, my eye, George. My eye's closing. See.

GEORGE:
We'll have it looked after at intermission. I have to go, Phil.

PHIL:
How do I explain this to my mother?

GEORGE:
Phil, listen. Just tell me one thing: can you go on? That's all I need to know.

PHIL: *leaping to his feet*
Oh, God, George, if that isn't pathetic. You have to ask Phil Mastorakis whether or not he can go on. And you want to know what's even more pathetic? I don't think I can!

PATRICK crosses to TOM.

PATRICK:
Hey, what the hell you doing? This's your baptism here tonight. Hold up your head, you're an actor.

TOM does.

It's not the end of the world. I don't hold it against you. Neither do the others. You know what happened to me my first opening?

TOM:
What?

PATRICK:
Nothing. It went like clockwork. I got a rave review....
Here.   *He takes out his pocket watch.*   Take this.

TOM:
I can't take your watch.

PATRICK:
I want you to have it.   *He drops the watch into TOM's hand.*   Think of it as a baptism present. My old man gave me that as a talisman the day I went into show business. He was so proud, the old bugger.

TOM:
Thanks, Pat.

PATRICK: *lifting TOM to his feet*
Besides, Tom, it could've been worse. We might've gone on tonight with Robert in the part. Perish the thought.

He sends TOM into the dressing-room.

TOM: *to GEORGE, showing him the watch*
My Dad didn't give me anything.

GEORGE:

Have a good show, I am everyone

> *As the actors make ready to go, GEORGE crosses into the Green Room to exit but is met by SUSI coming in; she puts her finger to her lips.*

Don't tell me. If it's bad news, I don't want to hear.

SUSI:

The baby-sitter just called. Your wife's in the hospital. She tripped on the way down the steps and broke her leg.

GEORGE: *leaning against the door*

Oh, God, I thought you were going to tell me Feldman couldn't make it.

SUSI:

You never let me finish. He just called from the airport. His plane was late getting in. Soonest he could be here, he said, was forty minutes.

GEORGE:

We can't hold the curtain that long. I don't care who he is. *Beat.* Can't he get here any faster?

SUSI:

He's just as upset as you are.

GEORGE:

Well, he'll have to see it another time. He can't judge the show on the last act.

SUSI:

Tomorrow's fine with him, he said. He sounded very nice.

GEORGE:

The actors won't like it. The second night is always a let-down.

The actors, aware that something is going on in the Green Room, are all staring in that direction.

SUSI:

Should I tell them? I don't mind doing your dirty work.

GEORGE:

Don't you dare or we'll have the let-down tonight. I wouldn't mind telling Patrick, only he'd never keep his mouth... *He puts a finger to his lips and crosses into the dressing-room. All four actors are staring at him.* Good show, everyone.

He raises his arm in a salute. Slowly all four actors raise an arm, almost in perfect unison.

GEORGE: *to SUSI, as they exit*

What hospital's she in?...

NICK: *over the PA*

Peggy, are beginners in place? It's two minutes to curtain.

JESSICA:

Two minutes? Oh, my God, what am I doing here? I could be home, knitting.

PEGGY: *into her headset*

No, they're not, Nick. Not quite.

NICK: *over the PA*

Actors, places have been called.

PEGGY gets her flashlight and crosses to the door that leads into the backstage area. She holds open the door and waits.

126

JESSICA:

I could conduct a better wig than this.

PATRICK:

Peggy, did someone turn the fan off? I'm not shouting above that racket.

JESSICA:

I think brushing only brought out the shine.

PHIL: *putting on his shoes*

A pair of shoes that don't squeak. Is that a lot to ask?

PATRICK: *flicking his lighter repeatedly*

I ought to tell George to stick this. What's he think I'll do, burn down the theatre? I'm bloody well insulted.

JESSICA:

I could've bought a wig myself. Why didn't I? *to PEGGY, plaintively* Oh, Peggy…

PHIL: *pacing*

With these shoes, they'll hear us going on in the dark.

JESSICA:

With this on my head, they'll probably see us.

> *By now all three actors are lined up at the door. PEGGY flicks on her flashlight and exits. TOM is seated at the make-up table, applying make-up between sips of coffee.*

JESSICA: *about to exit*

I don't know why she needs a flashlight. I give off enough light for all of us.

> *She pats her wig and exits.*

PATRICK: *shouting out the door*

Spoken like a true Star.

127

JESSICA: *poking her head back in*
Bet your ass.

    She exits.

PATRICK: *to PHIL*
Listen, mate, would it throw you too much if I use matches instead?

    He exits.

PHIL: *to TOM*
He doesn't even wait for an answer.

    He notices the shoebox. He snatches it up and rushes into the washroom, leaving the door ajar.

TOM:
Phil, what're you doing?

PHIL: *off*
Dumping his courage down the sink. That'll teach him a lesson.

    TOM closes the door so as to be able to inspect himself in the full-length mirror on the door.

NICK: *over the PA*
Okay, here we go. Have a good show everyone. Stand by. House to half. Light cues one through four. Preshow out and sound cue one.

    The doorknob rattles.

PHIL: *off*
Tom! Tom!

TOM:
What?

PHIL: *off*
I'm locked in! Oh, Jesus, Sweet Saviour, I'm locked
in! *He kicks and pounds on the door.* Get me out!

> *TOM rushes over and struggles to pull open the door.*
> *PEGGY darts back into the room.*

PEGGY:
What's going on? Where's Phil?

TOM:
In the can...

> *At that moment, the doorknob comes off in his hand and he*
> *goes backwards head over heels and knocks himself out.*
>
> *PEGGY rushes to TOM, sees that he's unconscious, and*
> *grabs her headset.*

PEGGY:
Nick, don't go on light cue one. Phil's locked in the
washroom and Tom's out cold.... Okay, I'll tell them
we're holding. *She rushes to the washroom.* Phil,
don't panic. We'll have you out in a jiffy.

PHIL: *off*
I'm too moved to speak.

> *PEGGY exits into the backstage area, closing the door*
> *behind her.*

Tonight was just not in the cards, Peggy. I know it
now. To have the critics predisposed against you is one
thing. To have Providence is quite another. He's in this
door, sweetheart. I believe that, within an inch of my
life. The God of the Old Testament. "Vengeance is
mine, sayeth the Lord."

As PHIL's speech continues, ROBERT rushes on and tries to revive TOM. First, he shakes him and then slaps his face, and then he applies the smelling salts. When this proves unsuccessful, he grabs the vase of red roses on JESSICAS's makeup table, but in his panic he gets the sequence wrong: with his right hand he hurls the roses at TOM, at the same time tipping the vase with his left hand so that the water spills to the floor. Frantically, he sits TOM up, trying to pull off his pajama top, at which point he notices the pair of striped pajamas on the make-up table. He lets TOM drop back to the floor and frantically tries to change into the striped pajamas. At the same time he has a script open on the floor, leafing through it in panic.

PHIL: *off*
The world is torn by chaos and strife. Nation against nation. Race against race. Religion against religion. Critics against actors.... My people created the theatre, bless their souls. Two thousand years ago. To celebrate the gods. To celebrate life.... *What* is He trying to tell us here tonight? I wonder, I wonder. Is He telling us we've strayed too far in the wrong direction? Telling us in His own inimitable fashion to get back to the celebration of life? If He is, amen to that. Amen.... Because Peggy, the human spirit is sacred and holy, a shining light in all of us. Disregard the nay-sayers, the cynics, the Philistines. The human spirit is alive and deserves to be uplifted and enshrined!

ROBERT: *one leg in the pajama bottoms and one foot on his script to keep it open as he scans the lines*
Phil, will you shut up! I can't think!

PHIL: *off*
You can't think? I'm only talking to keep my spirits up! You're not the one who has his foot stuck in the toilet!

TOM begins to stir and sit up as NICK rushes on carrying a fire-axe. RUBBER I MARRPS I I IVI AND TEARS NICK takes in the scene and grimaces with exasperation.

Blackout.

Music.

Act Three

The set of the play-within-the-play, the next afternoon around 1:30.

The stage still remains set for the last scene of the play from the previous night.

At rise, GEORGE and ROBERT sit at the table, working on the script, while PEGGY moves about setting up for the top of the play.

ROBERT:
Page sixty-five. Jessica's first line. I think it's weak.

GEORGE:
I like it.

ROBERT:
Wouldn't it be more effective to say nothing? That would make Phil work harder to reach her.

GEORGE: *wearily*
Cut it, cut it

ROBERT:
Not unless you agree.

GEORGE:
I agree, for Christ's sake.   *He strokes out the*
line.   But if it doesn't work, I'm putting it back in.

ROBERT:
Page seventy-three. Middle of the page. Patrick's second
speech.... George, the line is, "I went *towards* her and
she began to cry." That's much better than what he's
been saying.

GEORGE:
What's he been saying?

ROBERT:
"I went *to* her and she began to cry."

GEORGE:
"To" instead of "towards"?

ROBERT:
The rhythm is better.

GEORGE:
That might be tricky. He's gotten used to saying "to."

ROBERT:
You mean changing a preposition is going to blow his
performance?

GEORGE:
No, but it won't make that much difference, either.

ROBERT:
George, let a character use one word he wouldn't
normally say and I stop believing him.

GEORGE:

Listen, I've got to consider morale. If I keep harping on such minor points

ROBERT: *cutting in*

Minor points?

GEORGE:

Yes, minor points.

ROBERT:

To you it may be minor; to me it makes me cringe in my seat. And don't you think you ought to tone down his performance? It was way too big last night. I'm surprised he didn't get slammed by the critics.

GEORGE:

Robert, please. I've got enough on my mind right now. Give me a break, will you?

> *He picks up his script and crosses to the sofa and sits, exasperated.*

> *Just then, TOM rushes down the aisle. He carries a small brown paper bag containing a coffee.*

TOM: *thrusting the bag at GEORGE*

I'll never go to Luigi's again. That's the last time, George. He embarrassed me so much I went cross-eyed.

ROBERT:

Cross-eyed?

TOM:

Yeah, whenever I feel ridiculous I cross my eyes. To unfocus the world. You know.

GEORGE:

Why? What happened?

TOM:

He wanted my autograph.

GEORGE. *sipping his coffee*

Tom, you've just had your first taste of success. Learn to live with it. It's when they stop asking, you start to worry.

TOM:

I don't mind autographs, George. I hate actors who treat their fans with contempt.

GEORGE:

Why're you so upset then? I don't understand.

TOM:

He had nothing to autograph, so you know what he gave me?

GEORGE:

What?

TOM:

You know what he gave me, George?

GEORGE:

What did he give you?

TOM:

A menu. Like, he took a menu off the table and had me sign it. He even told me what to say.

GEORGE:

Well, to him it's a big deal. He'll take it home and show his kids.

TOM:

No, he won't. He put it back on the table. George, I know dozens of people who go in there every day for lunch.

ROBERT:
What did you write?

TOM.
"Hugs and kisses from the world's greatest actor, Tom Kent." I'll never live it down, George!

He starts to exit.

GEORGE:
Tom, wait a minute. Come here. I want to talk to you.

TOM returns.

Forget Luigi. Listen, what I'm about to tell you, I don't want you to mention it to Jess until I tell her myself. Okay?

TOM:
Bernie Feldman had a heart attack.

GEORGE:
Worse. He went back to New York this morning. One of his shows is in trouble. The way things look he may not make it back before we close.

ROBERT:
Two-faced little creep.

TOM:
Who does he think he is, the President of the United States? Even the President can spare a night at the theatre.

GEORGE:
I know.

TOM:
Doesn't he realize how much this means to Jess? Doesn't he care how hurt she'll be?

136

GEORGE:
I know, I know.

TOM:
Bernie Maple Leaf Feldman. He comes up here as if he's doing us all a big favour, and then pulls out.

ROBERT:
Coitus interruptus.

TOM:
He probably knocked up some showgirl and has to run back to get her an abortion.

GEORGE:
I know, I know, I know.

TOM:
Jesus, George. Jesus, Jesus, Jesus.   *He starts to exit and turns.*   Well, there goes my film career!

He exits backstage.

GEORGE:
He's going to make a wonderful actor, that kid.

ROBERT:
I know. He's got the right combination of empathy and self-absorption.

GEORGE: *to PEGGY*
Are the others here yet, love?

PEGGY:
It's only twenty-five after. They'll be trickling in soon. Robert, are you going to be long? I'll need you to move.

GEORGE:
We're almost finished, Peg. Just say the word.
to ROBERT   We *are* almost finished, aren't we?

ROBERT:

One more and that's it. Page ninety-eight. Bottom of the page, Phil's line. We don't need the line. It's subtext. Phil can act it.

GEORGE:

Great. His lines I don't mind cutting.   *He strokes out the line.*

ROBERT:

He's been screwing it up anyway. Last night his excuse was he had a hair in his coffee.

Enter PATRICK down the aisle. He carries a small thermos bottle and cup. He looks slightly hungover.

PATRICK: *sipping from the cup*

I take back what I've always said about critics. We're finally getting a few discerning ones.

GEORGE:

Congratulations. That was a helluva rave the *Star* gave you.   *He indicates the newspaper on the coffee table.*

PATRICK:

So Susi tells me. I've not read it myself. I just crawled out of bed.   *He steps onstage.*   Hello, Robert. What're you up to? Don't tell me, you've rewritten the entire first act.

ROBERT:

Have you really not read the reviews?

PATRICK:

Listen, sometimes I don't read them till the run's over. No, I mean it. I don't like to gloat. Irish coffee, anyone?

GEORGE:

Too early for me.

138

PATRICK:

Don't blame you, mate, it's bitter. Maybe I put in too much coffee. Oh, well. *He sits at the table.*
Speaking of last night, didn't you think that was a strange audience? A bit subdued? I think the house was papered with academics looking for meaning. Either that or Nick's entire family was here.

GEORGE:

I thought the audience was marvellous. Very attentive.

PATRICK:

Attentive is fine for a funeral. For the theatre I prefer wildly enthusiastic. And did you notice what happened to my only laugh in the play? Some old lady coughed right on the punchline. I could've strangled her.

ROBERT:

That was Phil's mother. She was chewing her worry beads.

PATRICK:

I might've known. I notice she never coughed once on *his* lines.

GEORGE passes the newspaper to PATRICK.

That's it, is it? *He begins to clean his reading glasses.* Too bad Feldman wasn't here last night. He missed a good show. The cast was in top form.

GEORGE:

Listen, Pat, about Feldman...

At that moment, NICK comes out from around the set, and SUSI starts down the aisle to the stage.

NICK:

Excuse me, George. I just did an equipment check. The Christmas tree lights aren't working.

GEORGE:

> How long will you be?

MILER:

> A few minutes. It's probably just the plug. *He sits in the window seat and repairs the plug.*

SUSI: *sitting on the arm of the sofa*

> George, Phil just called. He said to tell you he's just leaving. He might be a few minutes late.

GEORGE:

> We'll wait. I can't start without him. I need all four actors.

SUSI:

> You'll never guess where he's been all morning. At the hospital.

GEORGE:

> The hospital? Don't tell me his eye is worse?

SUSI:

> I was afraid to ask. I figured he'd never get off the phone.

GEORGE:

> How did he sound?

SUSI:

> Hysterical.

PATRICK:

> Listen, he's at the hospital more than the doctors. He's on a first-name basis down there. They set their watches by him.

SUSI:

> This was different. I've never heard him act so strange.

GEORGE:

How do you mean?

SUSI:

I could hear his mother in the background. And get this: he kept telling her to shut up and leave him alone.

GEORGE:

Oh, Christ, they've pumped him full of sodium pentathol.

SUSI:

It's out of character, isn't it? Let's hope he's not having a nervous breakdown.

She starts back up the aisle.

GEORGE:

That woman's going to be the death of him yet, I swear.

SUSI:

You think so? I have a hunch he'll get her first.

She exits.

PATRICK: *finding the review*

Don't you just love this? "*Roses* Author Has Green Thumb." Oh, that's cute.   *to GEORGE*   I don't know why but I always expect to get knocked by this fellow.

GEORGE:

Didn't you make a pass at his wife?

PATRICK:

Maybe that's the reason. No, really, he always gives me a rave, but in each one he manages to get in these little digs. Remember *Murphy's Diamond*? "Mr. Flanagan plays the baseball coach with a lustful twinkle in his eye and the smirk and leer of a perverted Peter Pan."

141

He glances at PEGGY.

PEGGY:
No comment.

PATRICK:
Okay, Patrick, settle down. Quiet on the set, please.
The modest actor will now read his glowing good
fortune, brief though it be... *reading* "Last night
a remarkable new play burst on the scene at the small
but prestigious Leicester Street Playhouse. Entitled *The
Care and Treatment of Roses*, it is the much-awaited second
play by Robert Ross, the young author of *Murphy's
Diamond*, the baseball play of three seasons past."

ROBERT:
Baseball play? It wasn't about baseball. It was a play
about a father and son.

GEORGE:
It was set on a baseball diamond.

ROBERT:
So what? Is *Hamlet* about castles?

PATRICK:
"The new work is old-fashioned in the true sense of the
word: well-written and well-structured, observing at least
two of the classical unities of place and action. The play
spans three days in the lives of its characters, and the
outcome is moving indeed. *to GEORGE* I can
see this is going to be boringly good. "Elizabeth
Thompson (Jessica Logan), newly-widowed, has taken a
lover (Patrick Flanagan), a violent and irascible
bartender, a widower who is haunted by the spectre of
his dead wife. With this simple situation the playwright
weaves a seamless fabric of passion and renewed hope
that threatens to unravel when her son, a college
student, decides to remain at home during the winter
break. The boy bitterly resents his mother's cohabitation
with this man and is intent on destroying the

142

relationship. He fails to understand her needs and the new lease on life that this vulgar opportunist symbolizes." *to himself* "Vulgar opportunist." Well, I suppose that's better than perverted Peter Pan." *back to the newspaper* "The play opens with Elizabeth and her lover, Frank, awaiting the arrival of her brother, Eric (Philip Mastorakis), a parish priest who has been summoned to persuade the son to remain in school. If there is a flaw in this play, it is simply that it begins too quickly. We leap at once into the conflict."

ROBERT:
What does he want, Ibsen? Two maids telling each other things they already know?

PATRICK:
"A more gradual build-up, it seems to me, would have worked much better."

ROBERT:
The nit-picking is just to prove he's doing his job. He can't just come out and say it's perfect.

PATRICK:
Right. "Enter the son (Tom Kent), the catalyst, who sets off the powder keg of conflicts. From the moment Mr. Kent staggers onstage, hungover from the previous night, the stage is set for a classic battle of wills, refereed by the priest—a battle that rages almost unrelentingly until the final curtain." *to himself* Ah, now comes the good bit. "The cast for the most part is superb. Patrick Flanagan as Frank, in the most impressive performance of his career, gives a tone and texture to his character that is truly breathtaking. There is not a false note in it. His final reconciliation with Elizabeth in the last moments of the play is the most genuinely moving moment of the night." *to GEORGE* I thought I was better in the last preview, didn't you? "Tom Kent in the pivotal role of the son, Jimmy, manages to strike the right balance between awkward youth and groping aspirations. A fine debut for

143

a young actor in his first professional role." *to*
GEORGE   Oh, that should please Tom. I'm glad he
got that "But by far the most memorable performance
of the night... *He pauses, his expression turning from
incredulity to outrage.*   ... goes to Philip Mastorakis as
the priest, brother of the much-put-upon
Elizabeth."   *to GEORGE*   "The most memorable
performance of the night"! We carried him the whole
night, the three of us.   *He tosses the newspaper to
GEORGE.*   Here, you read it. I can't read that
garbage.

GEORGE: *reading*
"But by far the most memorable..."

PATRICK: *cutting in*
Must you repeat that? That's only one man's opinion,
remember?

GEORGE:
"In a brilliant stroke the playwright has paralleled and
contrasted the groping of the son against the loss of faith
of this most human of all priests."

PATRICK:
He was so out of it before we went on I had to remind
him to check his fly.

GEORGE:
"Mr. Mastorakis, vulnerable in an almost painfully
childlike manner, fumbling for words that seem
constantly to elude his grasp, makes the inner struggle
seem all the more urgent and adds a dimension of
humanity that endears him instantly to the audience."

PATRICK:
You sure his mother didn't write that?

GEORGE:
"The only disappointment in the cast is Jessica Logan as
the doleful Elizabeth."

PATRICK:
    You're kidding

GEORGE:
    No, he hated her.

PATRICK:
    She was wonderful. No, I mean it. I wouldn't say that
    to her face, mind you. Christ, and he liked Mastorakis.
    Well, that just proves what I've been saying all along
    about critics. By the way, what does he mean, "the
    doleful Elizabeth"?

ROBERT:
    Melancholy.

PATRICK:
    That'll piss her off. All along she thought she was
    archetypal. What else does he say?

GEORGE:
    "Perhaps Miss Logan has been absent from the theatre
    too long. Perhaps she misjudged the intimacy of the
    small theatre. The fact remains that her performance is
    by far too large for such an intimate space, almost wildly
    extravagant, reducing the character at times to
    caricature. She starts off at such a high emotional pitch
    she has nowhere to go except into the upper ranges of
    hysteria."

PATRICK:
    God, that's dreadful. She'll be devastated.

    Slight pause.

NICK: *still working on the plug*
    Don't stop there, George. Read the rest.

145

GEORGE:

"For this, the director, George Ellsworth, must in part be faulted, although, otherwise, his handling of the cast is exemplary. Mr. Ellsworth has demonstrated in the past..."

PATRICK: *cutting in*

Don't tell me. "A fine and delicate touch."

GEORGE:

"... a fine and delicate touch, an unobtrusiveness that is the hallmark of a first-rate director. Perhaps Miss Logan was simply too strong a personality to control. That aside, *The Care and Treatment of Roses*, quite simply, is the best new play to arrive all season. And if it does not become the hottest ticket in town, this reviewer for one will eat his hat."

He tosses the paper on the coffee table.

PATRICK:

Eat camel dung.

PEGGY:

Typical. He didn't mention the set, costumes or lighting.

GEORGE: *to PATRICK*

The other papers are in the front office. You want to read them?

PATRICK:

What do they say?

GEORGE:

Basically the same thing.

PATRICK:

The answer is no. And to think I crawled out of bed for *that*.

He crosses to the armchair with his thermos and cup. He picks up a magazine and begins to leaf noisily through it.

PEGGY:

George, I'm almost through. I need the table now.

GEORGE:

It's all yours, Peg. And thanks.   *He crosses to the table with his script.*   Robert, give it a rest. Peg needs the table.

ROBERT:

I can take a hint.

GEORGE:

Why don't you use my office? Type some of these pages.   *He hands ROBERT his script.*   Only don't fuss with my desk. I like disorder. I'll never find a thing if you straighten up.

ROBERT:

Yeah, well, that clutter drives me crazy. At home I can't even work if the bed's not made.

He exits up the aisle.

GEORGE sits down on the sofa and sips his coffee.

PATRICK: *turning pages*
Phil Mastorakis?!

GEORGE:

I know. That should throw him into a tailspin. He's grown to expect the worst.

PATRICK:

I thought he was much better in *Titus Andronicus.*

GEORGE:

Are you serious? He was *dreadful* in that.

PATRICK:
    I know.

> *Enter JESSICA from backstage. She is bristling. As she
> strides on, she is swinging her wig. PATRICK buries his
> face in the magazine, and NICK, who is on his feet
> checking the Christmas tree lights, darts back into the
> window seat and pretends to be fixing the plug.*

JESSICA:
    Where's George? Ah, there you are. Stand up. I want a
    word with you.

GEORGE: *springing to his feet*
    How are you, love? What can I...?

JESSICA: *cutting in*
    Have you been in the dressing-room this morning? I use
    the term loosely. Black Hole of Calcutta's more like it.
    Even my roses wilted.

GEORGE:
    What's wrong with the dressing-room?

JESSICA:
    What's wrong? It *reeks* back there, that's what's wrong.
    The wallpaper's starting to peel from the smell of
    popcorn and cigarettes.

GEORGE:
    Popcorn?

JESSICA:
    Yes, popcorn. I know what popcorn smells like. Like a
    roomful of dirty socks. I defy anyone to go back there
    and not gag. Poor Tommy is face down on the sofa
    muttering "Jesus, Jesus, Jesus."

PEGGY: *to GEORGE*
    I haven't cleaned it yet. I was just about...

JESSICA: *cutting in, to GEORGE*
What do you take us for, a pack of degenerates? As if it wasn't bad enough before, being herded into a sweatbox, now you deny us a door on the WC. It's disgraceful.

GEORGE:
Nick, hasn't that door been replaced?

JESSICA:
No, it has not. Are you calling me a liar? And I want a fan back there to circulate the dust. You have one in *your* office, I notice.

GEORGE: *to PEGGY*
Leave that for now. Clean the dressing-room. Get someone to repair the door. And bring down the fan from my office. Right away.

PEGGY exits quickly backstage.

JESSICA: *to GEORGE*
Don't look at me like that. I won't be pitied or patronized. These are legitimate complaints, not the whimsy of some delinquent child.

GEORGE:
Sorry, love. I wasn't aware that I...

JESSICA: *cutting in and brandishing the wig*
And I won't wear this one more night, do you understand? Would you wear it? No, you're goddamn right you wouldn't. Yet you have the nerve to dress me up in a wig that any little street tart would think in bad taste. Well, I won't wear it.   *She tosses it at him.*
Take it back to the zoo where you found it. I play a housewife in this play, not Harpo Marx in drag.   *She turns and strides over to PATRICK and knocks away his magazine.*   And don't you ever hang up on me again, you hear? Don't you ever!

149

PATRICK:
Was that you this morning? I thought it was an obscene call.

JESSICA:
You're just lucky you took the phone off.

PATRICK:
Had I known it was you, love, I wouldn't have been that rude. I don't have any real friends. Only fans and enemies.

JESSICA: *starting to exit*
If I were a man, I'd take you outside and pummel you.

PATRICK:
If you were a man, I wouldn't go.

JESSICA:
Coward!

She exits.

PATRICK:
A rather weak exit line, I thought. Even Robert can do better.

GEORGE: *to NICK*
Why the hell wasn't the door put back on the washroom?

NICK:
The reason it wasn't put back yet is because we weren't supposed to have this illegal rehearsal, that's why.

GEORGE:
This rehearsal is not illegal.

NICK:
According to the Equity rulebook we need twenty-four hours to call a rehearsal after an opening.

GEORGE: *angrily*
You know what I'd like to do with your Equity
rulebook? *He tosses the wig to NICK.* The same
thing I'd like to do with your friggin' callboard.

*JESSICA comes storming back on. NICK exits quickly
around the side of the set.*

JESSICA: *to GEORGE*
I suppose you think I'm being a bitch, don't you? Just
because I demand to be treated like a human being.

GEORGE:
Jess, I don't think you're a bitch. I don't think that at
all.

JESSICA:
Well, I am a bitch, and you know why? I have to be to
get treated like a human being. So there.

GEORGE:
I see your point.

JESSICA:
What point?

GEORGE:
About being a bitch.

JESSICA:
So you think I'm a bitch, do you?

GEORGE:
No, no...

JESSICA: *cutting in*
I knew you did.

GEORGE:
No, I meant demanding.

JESSICA:
Oh, really?

GEORGE:
Yes, I think you're demanding.

JESSICA:
Why? Because I demand to be treated fairly?

GEORGE:
No, because...   *He pauses.*   Jess, I think I'm lost...

JESSICA:
What was I saying?

GEORGE:
Don't you know?

JESSICA:
Did you change the subject?

GEORGE:
What was it?

JESSICA:
I don't remember...

> *She sits on the arm of the sofa and lights a cigarette.*

PATRICK: *rising*
Excuse me, I have to call my agent. I'm the only one who ever does. It cheers him up.

> *He exits up the aisle.*

> *Pause.*

JESSICA:

Oh, George, I have the mark of Cain on me. In this racket that's worse than leprosy and twice as contagious. Aren't you worried you'll catch it?

GEORGE:

Listen to me. You are not a failure. Far from it. You bring more humanity to this part than any actress I know. You're just finding your level, that's all.

JESSICA: *pacing*

What's the circulation of the *Toronto Star*? You have any idea?

GEORGE:

Half a million?

JESSICA:

That many? Oh, God, half a million people who don't know my work now believe Jessica Logan to be "wildly extravagant."

GEORGE:

Jess, you were the one who asked for this rehearsal. Didn't you say last night you thought you were too big?

JESSICA:

It's one thing for *me* to say it, it's quite another to wake up in the morning and find it in print.

GEORGE:

I think you're overreacting.

JESSICA:

Yes, you can afford to be generous. They all *loved* you.

GEORGE:

What do you care about one or two critics? The audience adored you. They gave you a standing ovation.

JESSICA:

Be serious. Most of that audience was made up of relatives and well-wishers. They still hadn't read the papers to find out what they were supposed to think.

GEORGE:

That's a bit cynical, isn't it?

JESSICA:

I'm feeling cynical. My own brother saw the show and raved about me. This morning I showed him the *Star* review. You know what he said? "I didn't think you were *that* bad." George, I wasn't that bad, was I?

GEORGE:

You have never been bad in your life.

JESSICA: *still pacing*

To be the only one singled out. And to be drawn and quartered so brutally. "She has nowhere to go except into the upper ranges of hysteria." Anyone who didn't know better would think it was an opera.

GEORGE:

Jess, listen to me. The phone hasn't stopped ringing. The answering service is threatening to raise our rates.

JESSICA:

I'm not surprised. Opera is very popular.

GEORGE:

In fact, this show could be the biggest hit we've ever had.

JESSICA:

Do you know what I find so contemptible? The pomposity, the incredible arrogance. I thought only the Pope was infallible; at least with the Pope it's a Divine Right.

GEORGE:

Forgot what he said, will you? You're too good to take
that garbage seriously.

JESSICA·

I don't take it seriously, George, and I don't give a
damn *what* he thinks. It still hurts. We spend weeks,
months on a play to be carved up by someone on a free
pass who rushes home to scribble off six or seven
hundred words in sixty minutes that affects our
livelihood and reputation. I don't know about you, but I
can't even write a letter in that length of time. And oh,
his writing style, let's not forget that. He writes like he
needs a good enema. His sentences are so tight-assed, if
he ever left out a period he'd run right into Classified
Ads.

GEORGE:

That's all the more reason not to take him so seriously.
Who in his right mind would want to be praised by that
man?

PATRICK: *off*

Phil Mastorakis.

JESSICA: *as PATRICK comes down the aisle*

I thought you were calling your agent.

PATRICK:

The phones in the office are busy.

JESSICA:

Well, don't you disparage Phil. At least he has respect
for his fellow actors. He'd never deliberately make
someone look bad.

PATRICK: *stepping onstage*

I agree. By comparison he makes us look better.

155

ROBERT starts down the aisle.

JESSICA:
Is that why you got raves?

PATRICK:
Which makes me wonder why you didn't. Maybe in New
York you should play the Met.

Pause.

JESSICA: *quietly*
That's it. I quit. I quit, I quit, I quit.

GEORGE:
You quit?

JESSICA:
As of right now. You have my resignation. Effective this
very second.

*ROBERT sits on the edge of the stage and puts his head in
his hands.*

GEORGE: *in a panic*
Could we clear the theatre, please? Everybody out in the
lobby. I want to talk to Jess alone.

JESSICA:
Save your breath. I won't work with someone whose
tongue is sharper than his wit. Out of my way, Flanagan.
I'm in a very dangerous mood.

*PATRICK steps quickly out of her path as she exits
backstage.*

GEORGE:

Dammit! *then* What're you doing here, Robert?
Why aren't you up in the office?

ROBERT:

It's your wife, George. She just called from the hospital.
She asked me to give you a message.

GEORGE: *angrily*

What does she want now?

ROBERT:

A visit.

GEORGE:

Can't you see what's happened? I'm busy. I'll see her
tomorrow.

He exits.

ROBERT: *yelling after him*

That's it for me. I'm writing novels.

He steps onstage and sits on the sofa and taps his foot.

Pause.

PATRICK:

What're you trying to say, Robert? Get it off your chest.
I never did learn Morse code.

Pause.

So I'm the villain of the piece, am I? Is that it? Well,
don't forget: I made you what you are, you little bugger.

Pause. PATRICK sits at the table.

I was only kidding. I don't know why I even said it. I'm
just talking to hear myself. I've never liked being alone.

Pause.

How's your new play coming? You got a title yet?

Pause

Funny you should mention it, but I've been meaning to ask about *The Care and Treatment of Roses*. What precisely is the difference between "care" and "treatment"?

Pause.

Listen, she was just looking for a way out. You know that, don't you?

ROBERT:
Then why'd you give her one? Jesus, you're an actor. You know how vulnerable she is right now.

Pause.

PATRICK:
What'd you stop for? You have more to say when
I leave out a comma. Give me hell if you want. I know
you hate my guts.

Pause.

Listen, where do you get off blaming me? I'm the one who should be angry here. I'm the one she used.

ROBERT:
You?

PATRICK:
She baited me. You heard her. All I did was react like any good actor. Goddamn prima donna. I can act circles around her or anyone else in this country.

ROBERT:
Is that why you stay here?

PATRICK:
Just what does that mean? On second thought, keep your mouth shut. I don't like what comes out. *He stands and begins to exit.* And if you think you're such hot stuff, maybe New York's just what you need.

ROBERT:
Maybe it is.

PATRICK: *turning back to ROBERT*
How would you like to find out you're not as good as you think you are? As good as everyone says? Can you take that? Having your nose rubbed in your own worst doubts?

ROBERT:
I'm not afraid of it, if that's what you mean. *He turns to face PATRICK.* Listen, I want that experience. I want to be put up against the best. Otherwise, how am I going to grow, Flanagan? How do I develop?

Just then, JESSICA comes storming back on, carrying her make-up kit. Desperately, GEORGE runs ahead of her.

JESSICA:
No, I've taken all I care to take from that imbecile. I won't demean myself further. So goodbye.

She attempts to leave the stage but GEORGE blocks her way.

GEORGE:
Jess, wait, wait. Let's not be rash. I know you're upset, but can't we all sit down and discuss this like adults?

159

JESSICA:

We're not adults, we're actors. If you haven't learned that yet, you have no business in the theatre. Now get out of my way.

GEORGE:

Jess, without you in the cast this show will fall apart. I could never find a replacement.

JESSICA:

That's not true. I can think of any number of actresses who could do this part and better.

GEORGE:

Name one.

JESSICA:

Offhand I can't, but that's beside the point.

GEORGE:

Jess, this part was *made* for you. Robert practically wrote it with you in mind. Didn't you, Robert?

ROBERT:

Practically.

JESSICA: *indicating PATRICK*

I can't work with that man. He's the worst excuse for a human being that I've ever run across.

PATRICK: *to ROBERT*

I'll let that one go by.

JESSICA:

He's had my stomach in knots from day one. Oh, I can forgive his ill manners and his ill temper. I can forgive his vicious sense of humour. I can even forgive his alcoholic phone calls and his caravan of pizza trucks.

PATRICK:
How am I doing, Robert?

JESSICA:
But what I can't forgive is unprofessionalism. His behaviour last night on this stage was nothing short of atrocious.

PATRICK: *angrily*
And what was that, may I ask? Unless you're referring to my damn fine performance. In which case I stand justly accused.

JESSICA:
And you attack Robert for being ironic. My God, if that isn't ironic.

PATRICK:
How was I unprofessional?

JESSICA: *crossing so that she, too, is upstage of the table*
You know damn well what I'm talking about. *She sets her make-up kit on the table.* From the moment you strutted down those stairs you pulled out every stop. You snorted and bellowed like a wounded moose.

PATRICK:
I did like hell! *to GEORGE* Did I?...

GEORGE turns and walks up the aisle.

PATRICK: *to GEORGE*
I know I was rushing, but...

JESSICA: *cutting in*
Rushing? You were *charging*. The rest of us could barely keep up.

PATRICK:

Look, it was opening night. We were all nervous. Anyway, it's your own fault. You're the one who invited ⟨illegible⟩

JESSICA:

He wasn't in the audience.

PATRICK:

Did I know that? Every time I looked out I thought I saw him glowering. So maybe I was bigger than usual. A touch.

JESSICA:

Bigger?

PATRICK:

Must you repeat every word I say?

JESSICA:

The word is shrill. Shrill as in frightened silly. Shrill as in Irish soprano. And in half those scenes I'm supposed to top you.

PATRICK:

If we were both shrill, then how come only you got panned?

JESSICA:

Because I am the Star, darling. I am the Star of this goddamn show, and don't you ever forget it!

TOM rushes on from backstage. He sees what he thinks is the apron scene being rehearsed.

TOM:

Sorry, George. I fell asleep. You want me to get the apron?

GEORGE:

I don't think so, Tom. And I don't need you, either. We haven't started yet.

TOM:

Oh, I thought... Like, I thought...you know...

GEORGE:

I know, I know.

PATRICK: *to JESSICA*

Go ahead, tell the kid why there won't be a show tonight. I think he deserves an explanation. And don't use me as a scapegoat.

TOM:

There's no show?...

PATRICK:

Your mother just quit.

JESSICA:

I'm sorry, Tommy.

PATRICK:

The papers'll say, "For reasons of health." But we all know the real reason, don't we?

GEORGE: *from up the aisle*

That's enough, Patrick. Stop it.

PATRICK: *to GEORGE*

Then why didn't she quit last night? Why did she wait for the reviews? And why walk out the same day as Feldman is coming? Answer me that.

JESSICA:

Stop badgering him. What do you think this is, *Inherit the Wind?*

GEORGE:
Forget Feldman, the both of you. He's not coming tonight. He's gone back to New York.

PATRICK:
What!…

JESSICA:
I don't believe it…

GEORGE:
It's true. Ask Robert. Some crisis came up and he left.

ROBERT:
He has no class, either. He left the message with the answering service.

JESSICA: *to GEORGE*
Was this before or after the reviews came out?

GEORGE: *running down onto the stage*
Jess, for God's sake, stop believing the critics.

JESSICA:
Well, I don't believe there was a crisis. He just didn't want to face me, the coward. I'm supposed to be the draw in New York and I was the only one to get panned.

GEORGE:
Jess, this show's a hit. He'd be crazy not to take it.

JESSICA:
Oh, he'll want the show, he just won't want me.

GEORGE:
In that case, we'll find another producer. This play doesn't go to New York unless you go with it. Am I right, Robert?   *ROBERT turns away.*   I just don't want you believing you were bad.

JESSICA:

Bad? I was dreadful last night – and you know it. Godawful.

GEORGE:

You were not godawful, you were wonderful. All we have to do now is get it back to the right size. That goes for Patrick as well.

PATRICK:

Me?

GEORGE: *firmly*

Yes, you!

> *NICK rushes down the aisle. He is barely suppressing his indignation. He puts one foot on the stage.*

NICK:

Excuse me, George. I'd like to speak to the cast, if I may. Well, may I?

GEORGE:

Oh, be my guest.

NICK: *stepping onstage*

Now I'm not accusing anyone, I want you all to understand that. But someone in this theatre has taken a hammer and ripped the callboard off the stairwell.

JESSICA:

Someone stole the callboard? *She laughs.* Oh, God, there is a God after all. Wait'll I tell Phil.

NICK:

I'm sorry, Jessica, but I fail to see the humour. That callboard is there for a purpose. I want it replaced.

JESSICA:

Well, I'd like to take the credit. Believe me, I would.

NICK:

I'm not accusing you. I'm just saying I want it nailed
back up by eight o'clock tonight

JESSICA:

Don't you take that tone with us. You're lucky we don't
nail *you* to the wall. Now trot back to the control booth
and pull in your horns.

NICK:

Don't tell me what to do. You're no longer with this
show.

JESSICA: *crossing slowly to NICK*

Listen, you, I have never walked out of a show in my
life. The day I decide to let down my fellow actors I
guarantee you will be the first to know. Now stop wasting
our time. We've got a rehearsal to get through.   *She
looks over at GEORGE.*

Pause.

GEORGE:

Well, you heard the lady. We'll be starting as soon as Phil
arrives.

NICK:

Eight o'clock, George, or find yourself another stage
manager.   *He starts up the aisle and turns.*   And I
resent being made an ogre!

He exits.

GEORGE: *as he crosses and hugs JESSICA*

Thanks, Jess.

JESSICA:

God love the sonofabitch who stole that callboard.
*She glances at ROBERT, then at TOM, who shakes his head
vigorously. Slight pause.*   Thank you, Flanagan.

PATRICK:
>   Me?

JESSICA:
>   It was you, wasn't it? Who else is perverse enough to think of it, let alone do it?

>   *PHIL rushes down the aisle. His eye is swollen and badly discoloured. He is wearing an ascot, beret, and Hawaiian shirt.*

PHIL:
>   I'm sorry, boys and girls. I got here as fast as I could.

GEORGE:
>   How are you? How'd it go at the hospital?

JESSICA:
>   The hospital?

PHIL: *stepping onstage*
>   Ah, friends, you don't know what I've been through. No possible idea. I can't begin to describe it. Sheer torture.

PATRICK:
>   What were you doing, paying a bill?

PHIL:
>   That's exactly what I'd expect from you. No, I was not paying a bill. I was getting my stomach pumped.

JESSICA:
>   What!

PHIL: *nodding grimly to the others*
>   Incredible, huh? Fantastic.

GEORGE:
> Are you serious?

PHIL:
> Would I kid about a thing like that? You ever had your stomach pumped? It's murder.

JESSICA:
> No wonder you're pale. That must've been an ordeal.

PHIL:
> Tubes down the throat, needles, the works. I figured I was a goner. Food poisoning.

TOM:
> Food poisoning?

GEORGE:
> How'd you get that?

PHIL:
> George, that's not the worst of it. I just buried my cat, Gus.

GEORGE:
> Gus is dead?

PHIL:
> May he rest in peace.

PATRICK:
> Let me get this straight. You ate your cat?

PHIL:
> Very funny. No, my cat ate the tuna salad.

PATRICK:
> Then who ate your cat?

PHIL:

Anyway are the cat. What's wrong with you? Don't you ever listen?

JESSICA.

Phil, start from the beginning. We'll unravel it together.

She sits him in a chair at the table.

PHIL:

Okay. This's what happened. It's early this morning. Around seven. My cat's making noises. A wonderful cat. Like a brother. He's into the medicine chest, knocking pills in the sink.

PATRICK:

Does he do that often?

PHIL:

Every morning. That's how he gets me up. Intelligent, huh? I hurry down to the kitchen. I hunt around. No cat food. Nothing in the fridge but a bowl of tuna salad my mother made. I give Gus some and make myself two toasted tuna salad sandwiches on rye. To keep him company. Okay, he's finished. I put him outside on the porch and go back to bed. Around nine I get up, make myself coffee, and go out to get Gus.   *He chokes up.*   There he is, George. He's lying stretched out on the porch...

GEORGE:

Dead?

PHIL:

Stiff as a board.

JESSICA:

Darling, I'm sorry.

PHIL:

I panic. My first thought: food poisoning. I call an
ambulance and in no time I'm at the hospital. The rest
you know.

JESSICA:

Phil, that's terrible. What a trying day.

PHIL:

You think that's bad? Wait till you hear the finish. I go
home. I'm depressed, wiped out. My mother comes
back from shopping. "Oh, Phil, Phil," she says, "I'm
so miserable." "You think *you're* miserable?" I say.
"Yes, I'm wretched. I have a terrible confession to
make. This morning I backed out the driveway and ran
over Gus. I didn't want to ruin your sleep so I put him
on the porch." *He shakes his head
incredulously.* And she wonders why I'm mad.

PATRICK:

Phil, do you ever feel that life is making you the butt of
some vast practical joke?

PHIL:

Hey, what're you trying to do, make me paranoid?

PEGGY enters and continues her preset of the table.

JESSICA:

Yes, you leave my Phil alone. He got the best notices in
the show. Didn't you, my heart?

PHIL:

I was fortunate. Very fortunate, I must say. And what
they said about you, Jessica, is disgusting. I intend to
write a letter to the editor. Better still, I'll cancel my
subscription to the *Star*.

JESSICA:

That's sweet of you darling, but let's not get drastic, I'll tell you what you can do, though. Be brilliant tonight. We'll all be brilliant. To hell with Bernie Feldman.

NICK: *over the PA*

George, the rehearsal was called for two o'clock. It's now 2:05.

GEORGE: *to the cast*

Okay, let's settle down. This'll only take a minute. What we'll do today is start from the top. We'll run each scene individually and then work on it.

TOM:

Costumes?

GEORGE:

No, just props. I also want to work some light and sound cues. Does anyone object to that? No? Okay, then let's get this show on the road.

NICK: *over the PA*

Top of Act One in two minutes, please.

JESSICA: *taking TOM's arm*

Your mother doesn't have to wear her funny hair. Isn't that good news?

They both exit backstage.

PHIL:

George, I've been thinking. Maybe I should go back to the hairpiece.

PATRICK:

George, if Phil's getting his rug back, I want my adjustable lighter.

He exits.

171

PHIL:

George, can I have tinted glasses for tonight? It doesn't look right, George, a priest with a black eye.

He exits.

ROBERT: *rising from the sofa*
What about the changes?

GEORGE:

Later. We'll work them in during the run. Now is not the time.

He fusses with the set.

PEGGY: *to the control booth*
I'm all set, Nick.

She exits.

ROBERT:

Did you really mean that, George? You think we can still get this play done in New York?

GEORGE:

If not this play, Robert, your next. You've got your whole life ahead of you.

NICK: *over the PA*
He hasn't got that long. He has exactly sixty seconds unless he gets the hell off my stage.

PHIL rushes back on.

PHIL:

George, what's this I hear about Feldman? Are they kidding me or what?

GEORGE:

I'm afraid not, Phil.

PHIL:

Beautiful. Just beautiful. First the black eye, then Gus, and now this.

GEORGE:

What about that wonderful review?

PHIL:

A lot of good it does. I have to walk on tonight in those creaky shoes and shiny pants, knowing my future's back in New York with his feet up on his desk.

GEORGE:

Phil, we're running behind.

PHIL:

Look, couldn't Robert write me a line to explain the shiner? Maybe I got hit with a snowball on the way to the house.

NICK: *over the PA*

Forty seconds.

PHIL:

Incredible. I'm bleeding to death here, and that Turk is counting the seconds.

SUSI rushes down the aisle.

SUSI:

George, there's a call for you on line two.

GEORGE:

Not now, Susi. I'm busy.

SUSI:

It's Bernie Feldman.

GEORGE:

Feldman? What's he want now?

173

JESSICA: *off*
Tell him to go to hell!

PHIL:
Let's not be rash. Maybe he's had second thoughts.

SUSI:
He wants to know if you and Jessica can have dinner with him tonight after the show.

GEORGE:
Tonight? What do you mean?...

SUSI:
I mean he's still in town! He's at the hotel!

JESSICA: *entering*
He's not in New York?

SUSI:
No, and he says he has no idea who left that message on our service. Should I tell him yes?

PHIL:
Yes! Tell him yes! Tell him I'll personally invest in the Broadway show!

GEORGE:
Just tell him we'd love to have dinner. I'll call him back within the hour.

SUSI:
Gotcha.   *She starts up the aisle.*   Oh, and he says for the cast not to worry about the reviews. He never reads the local critics.

        She exits.

PHIL:
Terrific. The best reviews of my life, and the sonofabitch has principles.

JESSICA:

I knew Bernie would never desert us, George, I think we all owe that dear, sweet man an apology.

GEORGE:

I don't get it. Who would want to play a stupid sadistic joke like that?

NICK: *over the PA*

The same dumb shit who vandalized my callboard.

All eyes turn towards the top of the stairs.

JESSICA:

Flanagan, that was your cue.

PATRICK minces down the stairs, wearing an apron and JESSICA's wig, and carrying a red rose.

PATRICK: *mimicking JESSICA*

Honestly, you're worse than Jimmy. Your shoes are upstairs. And would you please put on a shirt?

JESSICA:

Why, you miserable, rotten—

She snatches the bouquet of roses from the vase and starts after PATRICK, beating him with the bouquet as he flees about the set. Pandemonium ensues.

GEORGE:

Jess! Patrick! Please! Please!

Blackout.

Music.